When college students begin disappearing from American campuses, a notorious cult, God's Delight, is the primary suspect. God's Delight has been hosting shows featuring sex, drugs, and rock and roll around the country, and young people are flocking to them.

Among the missing is the President's goddaughter, and he wants answers. When he asks Agent Cade Matthews, a member of a secret covert organization, to find her, the mission appears fairly straightforward. Find the God's Delight compound, determine whether a welfare check on American cult members is warranted, and get out. Simple. Clean. Easy.

Cade sends newly-married Agents Dianna Murphy and Anders Mark to the University of Wisconsin to follow the trail to God's Delight, but when they wind up in Bolivia, things go sideways. Suddenly, what appeared to be nothing more than a simple *in-and-out* could cost Dianna her life. When an Agency extraction is ordered, chaos erupts, and the question becomes, will anyone survive?

This book is a work of fiction. Names, characters, places, and incidents either are products of the author's imagination or are used fictitiously. Any resemblance to actual events or locales or persons, living or dead, is entirely coincidental.

Cult
Copyright © 2019 Seelie Kay
ISBN: 978-1-4874-2557-9
Cover art by Angela Waters

Published by eXtasy Books Inc or
Devine Destinies, an imprint of eXtasy Books Inc

Look for us online at:
www.eXtasybooks.com or www.devinedestinies.com

CULT
FEISTY LAWYERS BOOK 3

BY

SEELIE KAY

DEDICATION

To the survivors, the men and women who broke the chains of human slavery, and instead, fought for freedom.

CHAPTER ONE: THE ROOMMATE

Hope Ali stopped in front of the clothing boutique and pretended to study the ugly dress on the mannequin in the window.

Just outside of her peripheral vision, there was a quick flash of movement. Then it disappeared. Hope frowned. *Patience, girl. Patience. Make him come to you.* She continued to study the reflections in the window. *There.* The man in the black jeans and the Bucky Badger hoodie. He had been following her since she left the University of Wisconsin-Madison food court. While she knew Warren Hazelton, her bodyguard, had her within his sights, Hope had convinced him to fall back so she appeared to be alone. It had been a week since the man had begun following her. Today, she was bait. Hope wanted some answers.

Hope didn't know if she had an admirer, a stalker, or someone who had put a target on her back. She didn't really care. The man had pursued her long enough and she wanted it to end. It was the only way she could focus on what was important — getting her degree.

Unfortunately, past experience had taught Hope that she could never be too careful. Her parents were International Law attorneys who fought for the victims of terrorism. Her father, Sheikh Harun Ali, and her mother, Marianne Benson, were fearless and feared. They also had a price on their heads. The year prior, a terrorist posed as a high school student to get close to Hope with the intent of murdering her parents. Hope had almost become collateral damage.

1

She had fought hard to leave her well-secured family farm outside Milwaukee and attend college in Madison. After all, before she arrived in the United States, she had been educated at British boarding schools. She knew how to survive on her own. Her parents had finally relented when she agreed to round-the-clock surveillance. It was only for a year, after all. Hope had completed most of her college credits through high school Advanced Placement courses and online study during the summer. She'd have her degree in international relations by spring. Then she intended to disappear into the world of international espionage. *If the Agency cuts me some slack.*

Slowly, Hope stepped away from the store window and feigned disinterest. Her gaze remained on the window as she watched the man draw closer. Suddenly, she spun around and ran directly at the man. When she reached him, she swung her right leg and batted the man's legs out from under him. He fell and Hope slammed her high-heeled boot onto his chest. Bucky Badger—the University of Wisconsin mascot on his sweatshirt—appeared none too pleased.

Hope bent over and removed the man's wallet. In her cultured British accent, she crooned, "Hey, baby, perhaps you'd like to tell me why you've been tailing me? I know it's not because of my magnificent ass, though I couldn't blame you if it was." She flipped open the man's wallet and frowned. "Bloody hell! Why the heck is the Secret Service following me?"

The man groaned as Hope removed her boot from his chest and yanked the man to his feet. He was a little over six feet and lean. She gave him a stink eye and the man shifted uncomfortably. She held out her hand. "Weapon?"

"I can't—"

"You can if you don't want me calling the President and reporting that a nineteen-year-old college student, a foot shorter than you and half your weight, took you down. I suggest you cooperate. Now, hand over your gun or my bodyguard will search all of your . . .private parts. Thoroughly." Hope smirked.

Hazelton, a six-foot-four-inch former U.S. Navy Seal, appeared and pushed a pistol into the man's back. He laughed, a low evil laugh. "Wait until your buddies find out that you were taken down by a teeny, tiny woman. Geesh, where'd you train? Quantico?" His sharp blue eyes crinkled in amusement. He reached under the man's hoodie and removed a gun from his waistband. Hazelton made sure the safety was on and then handed it to Hope.

Hope took the weapon, shoved it into the back of her jean shorts, and adjusted her sweatshirt to cover it. Then she began to tap her foot. "All right, asshole. Explain why you've been following me."

The man flushed. "Damn you, Hazelton, put that gun down." He brushed his dirty blonde hair out of his brown eyes and studied Hope.

Hazelton kept the gun at the man's back. "What's the name on the Secret Service I.D.?"

Hope opened the wallet and studied it. "Daniel J. Perkins."

Hazelton withdrew his gun and placed it in his holster. He began to laugh. "Pesky Perky? No way." He spun the man around and studied him. "Shit, Pesky, you've been working out." Hazelton scowled. "Now why the hell are you following Hope?"

Perkins sighed. "The Ambassador sent me. Cookie Creighton is looking for a roommate. Hope was suggested. I was ordered to check her out, make sure it was safe to place the Ambassador's daughter with her."

"The U.N. Ambassador? Lydia Creighton?" Hope smiled. "She and my mom are friends. I met her last year. That hijacked plane she was on wound up buried in the cornfield next to our farm." She frowned. "Why would she be worried about me? She was right there when I took down one of the hijackers."

"Exactly. The Ambassador wanted to make sure that you don't attract trouble." Perkins shook his head. "Cookie has had problems staying on the straight and narrow. She was booted from her last two colleges. The Ambassador wasn't sure whether you'd be a good or bad influence." He glared at Hazelton. "However, since you hang out with a bunch of thugs, I decided a little reconnaissance was in order."

Hope giggled and nudged Hazelton with her hip. "Did you just call Hazelton a thug? He's been my personal body-guard since I was sixteen. He's the best, except when he chases away a boy who's interested in me." She smiled. "He's a little overprotective."

Hazelton smirked. "This from the girl who kissed a terror-ist last year."

"I didn't know he was a terrorist." Hope slapped at him. "And I didn't know he planned to shoot up my school. At least when he made his move, I got everyone out of my classroom alive."

Perkins gazed at Hazelton, then Hope. He sighed. "That's kind of what the Ambassador was concerned about."

"Oh, shut it, man. The woman is nineteen and smart enough to have skipped from high school straight to her sen-ior year in college. And as you just learned, for a squirt, she is quite capable of protecting herself. Cookie could not have a better roommate." He frowned. "The only question is whether Cookie is good enough for her? I don't want Hope stuck with some loser she constantly has to bail out of trou-ble. She needs to stay out of the limelight for her own protec-tion. You are aware of who her parents are?"

Perkins nodded. "Sheikh Harun Ali and his wife, Mari-anne Benson. Do you think Hope is still a target?"

"Not as far as I can tell. She's registered under a false name and has round-the-clock protection. Her building and her apartment are under surveillance twenty-four seven, plus she has a conceal carry permit and a black belt in several martial arts. Cookie couldn't be safer. Again, my worry is who she might bring to the party. The woman sounds like she might need a nanny." He scowled. "How old is she, anyway?"

Perkins frowned. "Twenty-two, but she's only a sophomore, due to all that flunking out."

Hazelton glared at the man. "You want to put a twenty-two-old dimwit in with Hope? Are you crazy?"

"She's not a dimwit. She has an I.Q. of 140. She just gets easily distracted by parties, booze, and men."

"Oh great, a nympho and a drunk. The answer is no." Hazelton scowled. "I am not subjecting Hope to that."

"Guys, I am right here. This is my decision, not yours. I don't have to accept any roommate I don't want." She smiled slightly. "However, it might be nice to have someone else to talk to, other than a bunch of former Seals and Special Forces types."

Perkins sighed. "Will you meet her, then? She has messed up in the past, but she seems determined to make this work. She has no choice. The Ambassador has reached the end of her rope. If she and Bucky Badger don't click, the Ambassador is going to cut her off."

Hope nodded. "I'll meet her for coffee. See what's what. But Hazelton is coming along." She pointed at Perkins. "And tell Cookie, she's buying."

Hope and Hazelton entered the campus coffee shop. After placing their orders with the barista, they turned to survey the other customers in the café. None of them matched Cookie Creighton's description.

Hope sighed. "Want to bet she doesn't show? It didn't sound like she's the most reliable of gargoyles."

Hazelton snorted. "I can't believe you just called her a gargoyle."

Hope shrugged and pushed off of the counter. She led Hazelton to an empty table. "Believe me, that was said in jest. I may need a gargoyle to ward off her type of evil." She sat and sipped her coffee. "Ten bucks says she doesn't show."

Hazelton smiled and tapped his coffee cup to hers. "You're on. Easiest ten bucks ever." He nodded behind Hope. "Perkins just arrived with a woman who looks to be the very definition of a Cookie."

Hope turned in her chair and waved at Perkins, then she studied the woman he was with. She looked like a debutante. Perfect long wavy blonde hair and large green eyes rimmed with what looked like false eyelashes. Her lips bore a garish purple lip stain and her cheeks were heavily rouged. "Oh, my God," Hope muttered. "Barbie in the flesh."

Hazelton grimaced. "Nothing like a tight sweater, knee-high boots, and a short, short skirt to qualify for the hooker version." He took a sip of his coffee. "Remember, you can say no. She needs your approval, not the other way around."

Hope nodded. "And it's not looking good. Not sure what an east-coaster is doing at a Wisconsin school, anyway. You'd think we'd be too lowbrow for the snooty types."

Hazelton studied her. "Seriously, Hope? Sounds to me like you think the fake princess might be too good for the real one."

"If you ever tell anyone that my dad is royalty, I will shoot your big toe off," Hope said, with what sounded like a hiss. "Now can it before they come over."

Hazelton took another sip of coffee, his eyes watchful. He

nodded at Perkins when he slid into the chair next to Hope and Cookie slid into the chair next to him.

Cookie handed each of them a scone. "I believe I was buying," she said with a smile. Then her gaze zeroed in on Hazelton and she batted her eyelashes. "Well, hello there, handsome. I hope you come with the apartment." She touched his arm and smiled.

Hazelton scowled. "Sorry, baby. I'm not in the habit of dating Barbies. I like my women smart, ambitious, and fearless." He removed her hand from his arm. "And no one touches me without my permission."

Cookie's lips pursed and then formed into a pout. "Sorry," she mumbled. "I was just trying to be friendly." She studied her coffee cup for a moment, then gazed at Hope. With an embarrassed smile, she said, "Hi, I'm Cookie. Guess I blew it already, huh?"

Hope chuckled. "Judging from that outrageous outfit and garish makeup, I suspect that was your intention." She cocked her head. "If I reject you, you'll have just another excuse for failure, won't you?"

Cookie's eyes grew wide. She sputtered, "What?"

Hope shook her head. "I've met your mom, several times. She's a cool lady, a real firecracker. Then again, as the U.S. Ambassador to the U.N., she has to be. Must be tough to live in her shadow." She sipped on her coffee and studied Cookie. "So, what is it? Are you screwing up intentionally, trying to embarrass your mom, or are you just a natural fuck-up?"

Cookie glared at Hope. Then she sneered. "Not everyone can be as perfect as you, obviously."

Hope laughed. "Oh, that's rich, deflect onto me. I'll bet you thought that a nineteen-year-old would put up with your crap." She frowned. "Why do they call you Cookie, anyway?"

"When I was little, my brother couldn't say my real name,

which is Catherine. But he could say *cookie*. The name stuck."

Hope tried not to roll her eyes. "And you allowed that?" She buried a laugh when Hazelton crossed his eyes. "So, here's the deal, *Catherine*. Ten rules. Take them or leave them, it doesn't really matter to me.

"No parties. No sleepovers. No booze or dope. Clean up after yourself. No distractions or disturbances when I'm sleeping or studying. No late rent checks. You buy and eat your own food. No borrowing clothes without permission. No hitting on my friends, and you follow Hazelton's rules as well."

Hope stood up and tossed her coffee cup into a recycling bin. Then she turned back to Cookie and grabbed her uneaten scone. "Your share of the rent is seven hundred fifty dollars a month. Your share of the security deposit is also seven hundred fifty dollars. We split utilities. You screw up and get kicked out, you continue paying rent for the entire term of the lease whether you're there or not. And I reserve the right to kick your sorry ass out if you turn out to be a raving bitch, a revolving door nympho, or an overall pain to live with."

Cookie huffed. "Need I remind you that I'm three years older than you?"

Hope laughed. A deep belly laugh. She swiped at her eyes, then shook her head. "And need I remind *you* that I am nineteen and a senior, while you're *still* a sophomore?" Hope motioned to Hazelton. "I need to get to class."

Hope led Hazelton out of the coffee shop. She turned to him and giggled. "Double or nothing. Twenty bucks, I say she runs. She doesn't strike me as the type who can follow the rules."

Hazelton rolled his eyes upward. "That's a sucker bet and you know it. Still, if she shocks us and accepts your terms, you may have your hands full."

Hope narrowed her eyes. "Oh, bring it on. I handled the mean girls in high school just fine. A self-entitled rich bitch is hardly a challenge. If she gets out of line, I'll just pistol whip her or tie her to a chair." Hope flipped her long hair over a shoulder. Then she cackled and walked away.

CHAPTER TWO: GOD'S DELIGHT

Professor Janet MacLachlan smiled at the students in her Constitutional Law class.

"And that folks, is why it is very important to understand what type of behavior meets the standard for impeaching a President. Article II, Section 4 of the U.S. Constitution clearly states *"The President, Vice President, and all civil Officers of the United States shall be removed from Office on Impeachment for, and conviction of, Treason, Bribery, or other High Crimes and Misdemeanors."*

Janet shut off the whiteboard behind her and turned back to her students. "Only Andrew Johnson and Bill Clinton have been successfully impeached by the U.S. House of Representatives. Johnson was impeached for dismissing Edwin M. Stanton as the secretary of war and Bill Clinton was impeached for lying under oath about his sexual relationship with an intern while in office. Neither President was successfully impeached by the U.S. Senate and therefore, remained in office. The only President in danger of being impeached and removed from office was Richard Nixon and he got out of Dodge." She smirked. "Which is why some called him *Tricky Dick*."

Members of the class laughed.

Janet sighed dramatically. "Look, many politicians are defective by reason of personality. I would venture to say that some of the biggest asshats you will ever meet reside in Washington, D.C. However, unless you can *prove*, not merely *claim*, that one of them is guilty of high crimes and misdemeanors, a charge of impeachment will not stand. They may be narcissists. They may be idiots. They may have offensive personalities, but that alone is not grounds for impeachment. You must have absolute, irrefutable proof that they have committed high crimes and misdemeanors. All of the hatred, histrionics, and violent protests in the world won't change that."

Janet cocked an eyebrow. "You do our constitution and this country a great disservice by claiming otherwise. Either we are a country of laws and we abide by those laws, or we submit to anarchy. And as lawyers, it's your duty to ensure that the rule of law always wins. We've survived two-hundred and forty-two years under our constitution. I am quite confident we will survive two-hundred and forty-two more."

She smiled. "And that, folks, is why you can bet a question about impeachment will be on my final exam." Janet smiled. "Class dismissed. Head outside and enjoy this beautiful fall day."

The classroom emptied until only one person remained in his seat. Janet walked up the steps, leaned over, and kissed him. "What brings you here, husband? I thought you were off to D.C."

Cade Matthews grinned. "Dianna and Anders resolved the problem without me. Not sure what happened on their honeymoon, but those two came back well-rested and raring to go. I seem to remember we were dragging for weeks."

Janet laughed. "That's because we got no sleep on *our* honeymoon." She ran her hand through her husband's long brown locks. "Maybe it's best you don't head to D.C. The President might force you to visit his barber again. And last time, that guy sheared you like you were a woolly sheep." She shuddered. "It wasn't pretty." She tugged at a lock of hair. "I kind of love this shaggy Alpha look."

Cade smirked at his wife, his green eyes filled with humor. "I learned my lesson. I was going to head to Harun's stylist on the way to the airport. I know how much you love *Sheikhie's* hair."

Janet laughed. "Mari complains it's too short every time he comes back from that woman. You two need to get a clue. Your hair can be a turn-on or a turn-off. I vote for the former." She grabbed his hand and pulled Cade to his feet. "Why the impromptu visit?"

Cade reached inside his jacket and pulled out an envelope. "This just arrived in the mail. I thought you'd like to open it." He handed it to her. "It's a present for you, Ethan, and . . ." he patted her stomach, which was well-rounded. "Our little sweet pea."

Janet took the envelope and withdrew a folded sheet of paper. Gazing at Cade, she smiled. "What is this? Are you going back to school?"

"Read it and cheer, woman."

Janet opened the letter and quickly scanned it. Then she burst into tears and hugged her husband. "How? When? With honors?"

Cade wiped a tear from her face. "Wow, those pregnancy hormones are fierce. Now I'm sure sweet pea is a girl." He grinned. "I let everyone think I was watching Sesame Street with Ethan while my leg was healing, but I was actually online finishing up the last few credits for my law degree. With a little Presidential intervention, I was permitted to monitor classes remotely. I wrote my last exam a few weeks ago."

Janet grinned. Cade and Sheikh Harun Ali had been seriously injured the prior year after rescuing the occupants of a hijacked airplane that had been buried in a cornfield. The terrorists had blown up the plane just as they were preparing to re-enter to remove one of the terrorists. Cade's shattered leg had kept him at home and in a wheelchair for almost nine months. "But why now?"

"I don't want my kids to think I'm a quitter or that I couldn't cut it at Harvard. I only dropped out of law school because I was fast-tracked to enter the Agency. Besides, if I'm going to require all of our recruits to have a law degree, I figure I should have one as well."

Another tear dropped down Janet's cheek and she hugged Cade. "I'm so proud of you. And you graduated with honors. Did you call Fred?"

"Are you kidding me? He called *me* when he heard I completed the last class. President Frederick O'Donnell wants to award the degree personally. In the Oval Office. I was just waiting for the paperwork." Cade grinned. "The President likes doling out special assignments, especially to me."

Janet kissed him. "Of course, he does, darling. And it doesn't hurt that you have a smart, sexy wife whom the President adores."

Cade laughed. "Noted. But no way is Fred pulling you into any more shenanigans. You stick to your hacking. I'll take the risks."

Janet smacked him. "The only reason I'd agree to that is because I am carrying sweet pea and I want to keep her safe. I can do just as much damage behind a computer as you can in the field."

Cade flushed. "I didn't mean to imply . . ."

Janet smirked. "Noted. So where to next?"

"Actually, the University of Wisconsin."

"Madison? Hope's there. Did something happen to her?"

Cade shook his head. "Hope's fine, but there's something going on that is concerning. Ever heard of a group called God's Delight?"

"No."

"It's one of those interfaith groups that flock to college campuses. They hold services and attract thousands. I guess it's a Woodstock format. Lots of music, free love, and a few illegal substances. Kids think it's a free concert, but it's much more. It's really a front for a cult. Five women have disappeared from the Madison campus over the past year and one of them is the President's goddaughter. None of the lettered agencies have been able to find her."

Janet frowned, "So? Sounds like a problem for the locals. Why is the Agency involved? Does it even have jurisdiction?" Cade worked for a covert organization so secretive its funding was listed in a U.S. Senate appropriations bill under the heading *Environmental Products and Services.*

"Well, God's Delight is suspected to be headquartered in another country, technically and legally out of the reach of most law enforcement agencies. However, since they also operate on U.S. soil, the problem of joint jurisdiction comes into play. The President wants it handled by one agency — less fuck-ups that way. Not only is the goddaughter in play, but more than a hundred other Americans are believed to have disappeared at the hands of God's Delight. And maybe a few others who fell through the cracks. We need to find the compound, then do a welfare check."

Janet's eyes narrowed. "That doesn't sound so hard."

"Maybe . . . Maybe not. If we find their headquarters, there's no guarantee they'll let us in to check on U.S. citizens. In another country, we have no legal standing. Cults know they can refuse and there's not a thing we can do about it. And we have to find proof that people are being coerced or being held against their will before getting any humanitarian groups, like the U.N., involved.

"The President is also worried about collateral damage. Remember what happened in Jonestown? After the government sent down a U.S. Senator and others to conduct a welfare check, Bob Jones lost it. Shot the Senator and most of the others in that group. Then he induced all of his followers to drink poison and follow him to the great beyond. Cults get paranoid when outsiders start poking around and some just start shooting. The President wants to avoid that kind of outcome. We need to get inside and find the missing Americans, determine if they are there, willingly, and if they're not, present the evidence to other organizations who have the authority to act. Under the new international human trafficking treaty, forced servitude, even in a religious cult, is considered slavery. Therefore, it's illegal and can be prosecuted."

Janet sighed. "And if they're there willingly, then what?"

"Then our orders are to walk away."

Janet snorted. "You realize, by definition, cults involve some sort of mind control, right? Whether the purpose of organizing a cult is religious, financial, or sexual, in most cases, they need to provide a reason for people to join and stay. Often, their purpose isn't enough to hang on to people, so there has to be something more, another incentive to hang around. And usually, it has less to do with free will and more to do with coercion. We're talking things that may be hard to identify at first, such as intense peer pressure, fear of isolation, paranoia, bribery, fear of safety, even drugs. A lot of times, even the targets aren't aware of what's going on."

Cade nodded. "I'm aware of that, but that's not our only concern. We're trying to determine how the students actually wind up at the God's Delight compound. We suspect that several college campuses serve as recruitment funnels. We're hoping to find the people involved and follow them to the cult's home base."

Janet cocked an eyebrow. "So, the funnel isn't the traveling shows they're doing?"

"As far as we can tell, that's just a way to build goodwill, a way to dangle the carrot. Soften up prospects. Make them more willing to hear the pitch. However, they are physically getting people to the cult compound another way. We're just not sure how."

"Tell me you're not sending Dianna in. I know she's the youngest and the one most likely to fit in, but after she was kidnapped by that slave trafficking cartel, she may not be the best choice."

"Dianna was cleared by the staff psychiatrists. She is mentally strong, with no signs of PTSD. Besides, we're sending her in with Anders. She won't be alone."

Janet glared at him. "You know as well as I do that a PTSD response can be triggered long after a traumatic event. You need to make sure Anders keeps a close eye on her and is willing to abort if necessary."

Cade smiled and kissed his wife. "Now that they're hitched, I think that's a given. Look how well I took care of you in the field."

Janet snorted. "That poor woman. No one to rely on but herself." Her eyes narrowed. "You're not targeting the UW campus because you're hoping to loop Hope into your crafty scheme, are you? Harun and Mari would skin you alive."

Cade laughed. "Hey, I'm bold, not stupid. We're convinced UW is one of the funnels. That's where the President's goddaughter was enrolled. So, we'll start there. If it doesn't pan out, we'll move to a different campus.

"As for Hope, she isn't part of the Agency. We only want to use her as an ear. She is not involved in any way, and no matter how hard she tries to worm her way in, her role won't change. We just want her to attend a rally or two, give us the lay of the land. Maybe identify some of the local players. We won't ask her to do anything dangerous."

Janet shook her head. "As if that makes a difference to Hope. She thinks she's *Wonder Woman*. If you get her involved, at any level, she'll jump in feet first and then you'll have to dig her out."

"That's why she has bodyguards. To keep her out of trouble. Besides, her roommate may lead us to God's Delight. She's been attending the rallies. If she gets pulled in, half of our work will be done for us." He cocked his head. "Guess who her roommate's mother is? The U.S. Ambassador to the United Nations. Lydia Creighton."

"Oh, no."

"Oh, yes. Our primary goal may be the goddaughter, but a secondary goal will be protecting Cookie Creighton from herself. The President is very concerned that if a cult gets its hands on the Ambassador's daughter, she could be used for blackmail or worse. So, the President has two cards in this game. Plus, more than one hundred other American citizens.

"That's why I need Dianna and Anders to take the lead. Hopefully, Dianna can bond with Cookie. Anders can be their wing person."

Janet cocked an eyebrow. "Almost sounds too easy."

Cade laughed. "And yet, those are the assignments that add years to my life."

Hope stood next to her roommate, Cate—the former Cookie—Creighton and studied the crowd around her. Between the live bands, free beer, and the overwhelming smell of pot, it was clear God's Delight knew how to throw a party. And while Hope didn't consider herself a prude, there was a little too much free love for her taste. Male and female students were engaged in all sorts of carnal activities with each other and the volunteers. *Didn't these people ever hear about safe sex and STDs?*

Suddenly, the band stopped playing and the crowd grew silent. A drum roll sounded. A tall, well-built man confidently strode out onto the stage and held up his hands.

Hope studied him. His hair was a dirty blonde and long, pulled back into a ponytail. His face was pleasant, more attractive than not. Striking blue eyes led to a strong nose and a wicked, full-lipped grin. Older than most in the crowd, he was obviously dressed to fit in. He wore torn tight jeans, a band tee, and bright red high tops, along with a leather tie at his wrist and a cross around his neck. He was hot in that bad boy sort of way. *All he needs to do is rip off his shirt, and he'd have the women in the audience throwing their panties at him.*

The crowd quieted. He smirked and the throng laughed. "Well, hello there," he drawled in a strong, sensuous voice. "For those who haven't figured it out yet, no, I'm not a roadie. My name is Reverend John." The crowd cheered. He ducked his head as if embarrassed, then grinned at the crowd. "I'm here to provide you with the way, the only way, to make the most of your life and walk with me into a glorious future. You see, you're young. People don't quite take you seriously yet. But you're already filled with a world of hurt, maybe even been subjected to all kinds of hate, wondering why the hell you're even here at all. Maybe you were bullied as a child or subjected to abuse. Maybe you've been subjected to racism or have been a victim of gender bias. Maybe your parents were so into their stuff they were never there for you." He paused and his eyes roamed among the crowd. "Maybe you just never felt like you fit in."

Some of the kids in the crowd nodded and he continued. "It's all bullshit, man. None of that crap matters. What matters is what's in here"—he pointed to his heart—"I'm not talking about the physical organ, but about your emotional heart and soul. How you view yourself, as a man or woman or something in between, the essence you want the rest of the world to see. You are in the process of becoming and I want to help you get there." He shook his head. "This is such a magical time for you, man. The world is just opening up to you. I want to be your guide. To help you to achieve your better self."

Reverend John chuckled. "I'm not here to perform miracles, to make a blind man see or a disabled woman walk. I won't claim to be the Living God—though I truly believe God speaks through me. I don't play those con games. I am merely here to offer you the opportunity to join my family— men, women, children, and others, who live and work together in unity and friendship, embracing a better life, preparing for that day when they cross the great divine divide and sit at the right hand of their God.

"Family should be the ones who accept you for what you are, who understand your potential and are committed to helping you embrace what you are capable of being. That's the opportunity I offer—a chance to step outside your normal existence and work with us toward a greater good. A world where people are encouraged to be who they are and become what they are meant to be.

"We live in a country filled with hate, replete with lies. I offer you a better way. I offer you true freedom." His white-toothed smile was dazzling. "Are you with me?"

Many in the crowd yelled, "Yes!"

"Then walk with me. I will show you that life can be filled with love and laughter. That as a family, we can all reach a better place." Reverend John opened his arms wide, his expression intense. "I embrace each and every one of you, with all of your quirks, foibles, or imagined shortcomings. In my family, we love one another unconditionally and I want to share that love with you. I don't care about race, gender, socioeconomic status, or religion. You are part of us now and I welcome you to my family."

Reverend John handed the mike to a roadie and walked off the stage. The crowd erupted with applause and whistles. Another man took the stage and began to share his personal experiences with God's Delight.

Hope took a long sip of water, her gaze darting among the crowd. It was the perfect pitch for college students, people feeling uncertain and afraid about what lay ahead. And it offered just the right touch of adventure for those wanting more. Hope tried not to show her disgust. *I am so not into this type of existential bullshit. Maybe I'm just too much of a realist. Heck, I know how ugly the world is. I've been kissed by a terrorist and targeted by kidnappers. Sometimes, reality bites. You learn to deal with it.*

Hope turned to Cate. Clearly, she was into the whole Reverend John scene. This was her third visit to one of his rallies. Cate had spent most of the concert making out and being groped by random strangers—in between gulping down plastic cups of beer handed out by God's Delight volunteers. However, when Reverend John spoke, Cate had quieted. She listened reverently. Her face filled with adoration. She appeared enraptured by the revival tent preacher. Sure, the man gave off those sex-on-a-stick vibes, but his message was nothing creative or new. It simply targeted the very people most vulnerable to that kind of crap. College students.

A volunteer walked up to Cate and whispered into her ear. She grinned and started to jump up and down.

Hope studied her. "What?"

Cate leaned over and slurred, "I get to meet the big guy, Reverend John." She squealed. "I can't wait."

Hope tried not to frown at her roommate. She forced herself to nod. "Okay, then. I'm going to head out. Call me if you need a ride."

Cate gave Hope an exuberant wink. "Don't wait up. And if I don't make it home, don't worry. I've been chosen to attend a private prayer session." She giggled. "God only knows what that entails." She wiggled her butt. "Sounds like a booty call to me. I'm so glad I wore my favorite thong."

Hope sighed, then turned away. For the most part, Cate

had kept it together since arriving on campus and moving into her apartment. She had engaged in the occasional hookup, but always away from her place. She hadn't really witnessed Cate's wild side until the God's Delight concert.

Because Hope was underage, she had never accompanied Cate on any of her forays into the area nightclubs and taverns, but Cate always shared every last detail the morning after. Being the younger of the two, Hope had withheld her opinion that Cate was a stone-cold slut. However, she did worry that one day Cate's promiscuousness would bite her in the ass. Hooking up with a hot forty-year-old traveling preacher just seemed like a recipe for disaster, but Hope knew it wasn't her place to object. Instead, she quickly hugged Cate and walked away.

She discreetly nodded at Hazelton, who stood along the side of the large meeting hall, and walked to the main door. After a minute, he followed. When they walked out into the parking garage, Hazelton asked, "Cate's not coming back with you?"

Hope shook her head. "A volunteer invited her to a private prayer session, whatever that means. I promised her a ride if she needed one, but I'm guessing she won't grace my door until sometime tomorrow. And since we're headed to the family farm in the morning, I probably won't see her until Sunday night."

Hazelton emitted a slow whistle. "Wow, that one's certainly not afraid to take a walk on the wild side."

Hope shrugged. "She's an adult and responsible for her own choices. However, I think Ambassador Creighton is right to be concerned. That girl is so reckless sometimes, it's scary."

Hazelton cocked an eyebrow. "So, it's time to cut her free?"

Hope winced. "God, I feel like such a bitch for even thinking that. I'm willing to give her a few more weeks. See if she settles down. Cate's nice enough, just a little too wild for my tastes. As long as she doesn't bring it to my door, I really shouldn't complain. Who knows, by then Cate might move on without a push from me. She might even join God's Delight."

"Or she'll get scared straight. Getting it on with a forty-year-old preacher is kind of creepy, especially since the guy probably has a girl in every port." He shook his head. "Not smart."

Hope giggled. "You're just upset she's no longer drooling all over you."

Marianne Benson stared at her daughter, her expression appalled. "Cookie is doing what?"

"Mom. She's twenty-two. Technically she's an adult." Hope sat on a stool by the kitchen counter as Mari prepared breakfast. "It's not like we are buddies or anything. That girl just plunges through life and *damn* the consequences. I figured the smartest thing to do was simply get out of her way. Besides, I would be surprised if she survived the semester."

Mari groaned. "Lydia is going to be so ticked. That girl has given her nothing but trouble. She's just a disaster waiting to happen. If she joins that cult, she will not only put herself in peril, she puts the Ambassador and everything she has worked for at risk." Mari shook her head. "My understanding is that God's Delight has some connections to Latin America, and that could mean anything. My greatest fear, though, is that Cate is putting herself out there as bait for kidnappers or traffickers . . . anyone likely to comprehend what a lucrative pay-off she could provide."

She gazed at Hope. "What are the requirements for joining this cult? Give up all your worldly goods? Work to pay your own way?"

Hope shook her head. "That's what I don't get. There's none of that. As far as I can figure out, you live with others as family and volunteer to work in areas that support the family, like farming, construction, housekeeping, teaching. Wherever the compound is—and they didn't say—they are self-sufficient and self-supporting. They even offer the opportunity to visit the compound for a week, to determine whether it's right for you."

"So, no standing on street corners, knocking on commuter windows, selling flowers?"

Hope shook her head. "Nope. As far as I could figure out, you're free to leave or stay, with no consequences."

A bemused look crossed Mari's face. "It almost sounds like the communes in the 60's—sex, drugs, and rock n' roll. Hardly a new concept, but I imagine for someone who is dissatisfied with their life, it's an attractive one. It's so easy for a certain type of person to fall into that. And the danger lies in becoming involved in an organization that takes away your free will. A group that controls your decisions and your life." She shuddered. "Cults are so insidious, and we've witnessed the damage they do—Jonestown, the Moonies . . . People worshipped the leaders without question and lost so much. That's what makes God's Delight so darn scary."

Hope strolled into her apartment Sunday evening and called out for Cate. She got no response. She checked in Cate's bedroom, but the bed, while unmade, was empty. However, the outfit Cate had won on Friday was crumpled up on the floor, so Hope knew she had made it home, at least once.

Hope dumped her duffle bag onto her own bed and headed for the kitchen. She came to an abrupt halt when she spotted a leg hanging over the side of the living room couch.

Hope moved closer. "Cate? Are you okay?"

Cate moaned and moved a leg. She tried to sit up, then fell onto her back. She grabbed her head and groaned. "That man's a sex machine." Cate opened her eyes then snapped them shut. She groaned. "Between the drugs and the booze, everyone was pretty wild. And he expected me to join right on in. Twosomes, threesomes . . . Somehow, I managed to get out of there, snagged an Uber, and headed home."

Tears began to spill out of her eyes. "God, everything got so out of control. I was so stoned. Hell, I might have even been roofied. There's so much I don't remember. I could not believe the stuff they were passing around." She groaned again. "God, I hope there are no photos. My mother will be livid."

Hope frowned. "Um, maybe you should get checked out? Get tested?"

"Student Health's not open for anything but emergencies until Monday. I checked. I'll go then. Meanwhile, every inch of my body hurts." Cate moaned.

"So now what?"

Cate flapped her hand. "The Reverend called all week-end. For some reason, he thought I'd be up for a road trip. I finally blocked him. I hope that's the end of it. He was heading to Detroit today. He's gone."

Hope shook her head. "Well, thank God for small favors."

CHAPTER THREE: GOOD OLD-FASHIONED POLICE WORK

Cade and the junior members of his team, Anders Mark and Dianna Murphy, gathered in front of a whiteboard in an unmarked government office on the UW-Madison campus and studied the information that had been posted.

Cade nodded at the photo of Reverend John. "Note all of that guy's aliases. His real name is John Robert Thompson, also known as The Right Reverend Archbishop John, Master John, and now, Reverend John. I don't think this is his first rodeo, just the most successful one. No record of a divinity degree. Never served as a pastor of any kind to any congregation. In fact, the guy has an undergraduate degree in fine art." Cade walked back to a console and called up another document. "The only priors we could find were for misdemeanors, such as disturbing the peace, public intoxication, and indecent exposure."

Dianna cocked an eyebrow. "Indecent exposure? For what?"

Cade smirked. "Mainly for urinating in public. Guy doesn't hesitate to drop trou when he has to whiz. However, one of those charges was for fornicating in public with this woman." He waved his hand over the console and a photo of a young woman with long dark hair and brown eyes popped up. "This is Sister Bethany. Supposedly his right-hand woman. Also, allegedly his wife, though no marriage records could be found. Rumor has it they married on a moonlit hill somewhere in California. No witnesses. Reverend John performed the ceremony himself."

Anders smiled. "How practical. If they ever split up, there's no need for a divorce because the marriage was never legal in the first place. Though that also means Sister Bethany gets none of his riches. You can bet he keeps everything in his name."

Cade nodded. "Well, she's hanging in there for now. Supposedly, she's in charge of procuring women for their road trips. There's lots of free love flowing in God's Delight."

Dianna gazed at Cade, her big, blue eyes puzzled. "So, it's a sex cult? Not a religious one?"

Cade sighed. "We're not sure. Typically, sex cults are smaller and are mostly comprised of women, with a few men who lead. Much like a harem. It's about sex and only sex. From everything we've been able to learn, this group promotes themselves as family—a fully-functioning commune. Free love, for the most part, but only a small group of women appear to consistently service Reverend John."

Anders raised his eyebrows. "So, what's the problem?"

Cade sighed and swiped his hand over something on the console. A photo of a brown-haired, brown-eyed woman with a toothy grin popped up. "This is Meredith Wright, Merry to her friends. She disappeared from the UW campus six months ago. Friends claim she was heading out of the country with a student group to do some sort of missionary work. Before she disappeared, she was seen attending rallies for God's Delight and appeared to be intimately acquainted with the good Reverend."

"So, she went on the road with them?" Dianna asked.

Cade shook his head. "That's where things get confusing. There is no evidence of that. But we also were unable to find out what student group she left with or where she went. All we know is she never returned. However, she's also the President's goddaughter. He wants her found and, if warranted, returned to the U.S. Unfortunately, she's only a small part of the problem." Cade hit a button on the console and the whiteboard filled with photos of multiple young women and men. "Other students are disappearing from college campuses around the country, all with the similar back stories. Mostly female, as you can see, but some males as well."

"Is the connection between God's Delight and the missionary trips firmly established or merely a suspicion?"

Cade shook his head. "All we have right now is circumstantial evidence. College students take missionary trips all the time. That's nothing new. However, in the case of these missing college students, most had also expressed an interest in God's Delight at some point. Unfortunately, the trail pretty much ends there. The missing students shared almost no information on where they were headed, other than South America. We're not even sure who they went with. By the time the students were reported missing, the trail was cold."

Dianna asked, "Any evidence they actually left the country?"

Cade shook his head. "If they did, they didn't go out legally. ICE has no record of any of them leaving and if they had passports, none were used. Similarly, an international check revealed no evidence that they had entered another country."

Dianna frowned. "Which means they could be alive, dead, in prison, or, well, anywhere really."

"That's what's so troubling. We know that some went alone and were joining up with others, or actually traveled in groups, but we haven't been able to pin anything down. Without the passport information, we can't know who they traveled with or where."

Anders scratched his head. "That's just odd. Regular airlines check passports. So maybe the groups used private charters? Or maybe someone hacked into the airline reservation system and erased names? There has to be something else that connects these people."

Janet MacLachlan walked into the room. "Maybe, but it's not definitive. Many of the missing had some sort of affiliation with the Greeks." She pushed a button on the console and a graph popped up.

A confused expression crossed Anders' face. "The Greeks? Why would they have something to do with it?"

Dianna shook her head. "Not people from Greece, silly. People who are in sororities and fraternities."

Anders flushed. "Got it. Been there, done that." He studied the chart. "Not all of the people have fraternity or sorority designations, though."

Janet nodded. "However, many do. And there are other ways to get drawn into that world without actually joining a sorority or fraternity. The parties thrown by the fraternities are usually open to anyone on campus, not just the Greeks. Friends, people they want to recruit, hot girls. If any of those houses are serving as funnels or feeders, they have access to other students. The stats don't include everyone, but there are enough connections to raise suspicion. Over fifty percent of the people who disappeared were linked to a fraternity or sorority. That's significant."

Dianna studied the list. "You need little sisters on the list as well."

Cade frowned. "What?"

"Fraternities have what they call *little sister* programs. They invite all the pretty girls to hang out at their houses, help out with fundraisers, and attend parties. You don't have to be a Greek to be a little sister. There are a lot of women without Greek designations who are little sisters."

Anders gazed at Dianna. "And you know this, how?"

Dianna shrugged. "I *was* a little sister."

Anders laughed and shook his head. "Of course, you were."

Dianna glared at her husband and her eyes narrowed. "What's that supposed to mean?"

"Just that I imagine almost every fraternity wanted you as their little sister. You're one hot woman." He smiled. "If I had been in college with you, I would have followed you around like a puppy dog."

Dianna punched him. "Stop it. I married you because you didn't drool."

Cade laughed. "First fight, folks?"

Dianna snickered. "That doesn't even rise to a fight. When we fight, you'll know it." She pulled Anders' tall body against hers and stood on tip-toe to kiss him. Then she pointed at the whiteboard. "We need to find out if any of those women were little sisters." Her eyes lit up. "Maybe I can go undercover as a little sister again." She clapped her hands in mock delight. "Oh, goodie, cheap beer, crappy music, and smelly guys."

Janet smirked. "Ah, the good life. Still, the little sister angle should be easy enough to follow up on." She gazed at Cade. "If you can lend me a few interns, I can wrap that up today."

"And how will you do that?" Anders asked. "It's not exactly something you put on your resume."

"The same way we do everything else," Janet replied. "We call their families and ask. Good old-fashioned police work."

Cate rushed into the apartment, her face flushed with excitement.

Hope turned to her and smiled. "Someone's happy today.

What's up?

Cate bounced on her toes. "I got an invitation to be a little sister at Tau Omega Psi."

Hope frowned. "Tau what?"

Cate giggled. "It's a fraternity, silly. I went to one of their parties last Friday and, today, the members invited me to be their little sister." She clapped her hands. "I'm so excited. That means I'll be invited to all the best parties. And they have a spring formal that is absolutely mag. They spend big bucks and do it up right. It runs an entire weekend. They always hold it at a resort."

Hope tried not to roll her eyes. "So, what do you have to do to be a little sister?"

"Show up at parties, help with fundraisers. Sometimes serve as dates for members for important events. Nothing too taxing." She clapped her hands, again. "I have the best idea. Why don't you come to the next party with me? Maybe you'll meet someone. You know, to date." She squealed. "And maybe you could become a little sister, too."

"First of all, I'm not exactly in the market for a boyfriend. I don't have time."

Cate studied her. "You're not gay, are you?"

Hope laughed. "Now that's a stretch. I've had boyfriends. I just don't have the time. I want to get my coursework done and graduate. And that means hitting the books at every opportunity."

"But you're so pretty. The guys would love you. Come with me to one party, please."

Hope tried to hide her disinterest. "Cate, I'm underage. They card at those things. I'm nineteen, two years away from the legal drinking age. Jail bait."

Cate's eyes narrowed. "That's just an excuse. It would be easy to get you a fake I.D. Heck, I doubt the guys even care."

Hope glared at Cate. "Well, I care. I'm not about to get

kicked out of college for underage drinking. I have plans, and they don't include a misdemeanor on my record."

In a sing-song voice, Cate replied, "I'll just keep asking until you cave. Easy-peasy." She giggled.

Hope rolled her eyes again and went back to her textbook.

Dianna pointed at the line item on the whiteboard that had been added to the graph for known and suspected recruits for God's Delight. "Can you segregate the ones who were little sisters by fraternity and university?"

Janet nodded and pushed a button on the console.

Dianna grinned. "We have a winner! Look at the number of women who were little sisters at Tau Omega Psi from UW-Madison. More than three-quarters of the women missing on that campus. That can't be a coincidence."

Janet nodded. "That doesn't necessarily mean that Tau Omega Psi is doing the recruiting, though. Someone could be targeting their parties to find prospects. As I recall, fraternities throw some pretty wild parties. Along the lines of that old movie about a frat house that got banned on campus. Ohhh, what's the name of it?" She nudged Cade. "You know, the one with those two comedians? The Blues Brothers."

Cade chuckled. "I believe you mean *Animal House*, darling."

Anders and Dianna appeared confused. Finally, Dianna asked, "Um, how old is this movie?"

Janet flushed. "Oh, shush. It was even before my time. I saw it on an old movie channel. Besides, you're missing the point. They're party boys. That's where we should start. Their parties. Considering how much liquor is consumed at those things, it should be pretty easy to figure out if anyone stands out."

Anders cleared his throat. "Actually, I was a member of that fraternity at one time, but at Duke." He flushed. "Sorry, I didn't really want to disclose that. I was hoping another frat would be involved. I grew up. Left that shit behind. Anyway, I have an alumni connection and that means I have reason to stop by and hang out. I could even stay at the house. However, I'm a bit too old to pass myself off as a student."

"We'll need a backstory for your presence there, then." Janet smirked. "You could go undercover as a tax lawyer getting an advanced degree."

Dianna hooted. "Married to a tax lawyer. Oh, kill me now!"

Anders scowled. "How long do I need to be there? If it's only a few days or weeks, I'm sure I could find some sort of continuing legal education course to attend. I could claim I got behind in my legal education credits and am playing catchup. Heck, I probably am behind. I need to earn thirty credits every two years and I've done nothing thus far. This is the time of year when they offer those mega-credit workshops for slackers. I don't even have to attend. I could just show up, pick up the materials, and leave."

Cade snickered. "Or you could actually go . . . You'll have to pay for those classes and if you want the government to reimburse you, you're going to have to prove you attended."

Anders waved him off. "Fine."

"Now we need to figure out how to get Dianna in as a little sister." Janet considered. "Hope's underage. Technically, she can't even attend those parties. Her roommate is of age, though, and from what Hope has told us, quite the party girl. Maybe Hope could introduce Dianna as a cousin or family friend. Then Dianna could ask Cate to show her around. Suggest they hit the party circuit. In particular, Tau Omega Psi."

Cade nodded. "However, I want Dianna in classes, too, maybe as a transfer student. She needs to be seen around campus. She is going to get lots of attention." He smirked at Anders. "Sorry, mate. A little buzz won't hurt efforts to get her in at Tau Omega Psi. There might even be some competition for her attention."

Anders glared at Cade.

Janet quickly offered, "Maybe Dianna could bunk with Hope. I know she has an extra bed. Originally, the Ali's rented a multi-bedroom suite for Hope, thinking one of the security guys would be staying there. Eventually, however, they decided that was too obvious. Instead, they opted for video surveillance. This could provide Dianna with an opportunity to forge a stronger connection with Cate."

Anders groaned. "So, my wife won't even be living with me?"

Dianna laughed. "Well, I'm certainly not living at a frat house. They'd expect me to do their laundry and clean up after them." She shuddered. "That is so not happening." Then her eyes grew wide. "Oh, shit. That's what little sisters do."

Janet grinned. "Better you than me. I've got potty training for a two-year-old and impending birth on my plate." She patted her stomach. "No way I'd pass for a co-ed in this condition." Janet cracked her knuckles. "But I am always available for hacking, safecracking, and related activities."

CHAPTER FOUR: THE SISTERHOOD

Dianna placed a duffel bag at her feet and knocked on the apartment door.

Hope opened the door wide and smiled. "Bennie!" she exclaimed. "I'm so happy you're here!"

After much discussion, the Agency had decided to keep Dianna's undercover tag as close as possible to her real name. Since her middle name was Bernadette, she became Bennie. And her new last name, Mark, was changed to Marks.

Hope had been filled in on her undercover identity and her role the week before. Because Hope's dark hair, eyes, and skin sharply contrasted with Dianna's blonde hair and blue eyes, they decided Dianna would claim to be the daughter of a family friend. Together, Dianna and Hope had built a cover story that was believable but also required knowledge of a minimal amount of information. To everyone else, Bennie was a transfer student in need of temporary housing. Hope just happened to have an extra room.

Hope pulled Dianna into the apartment. "Come meet my roommate." She turned to Cate, who was sitting at the kitchen table eating a toaster waffle.

Cate waved, waffle in hand. "Hey, Bennie." She studied Dianna and her eyes narrowed. "I was expecting someone Hope's age. You look to be my age. Are you legal?"

Dianna smiled. "Yes, and I have been for a year. You?"

"Same." Cate sighed dramatically. "Please, please, please tell me you like to party. The young one here doesn't even drink."

Dianna shrugged. "Sure. Though I have to watch it. Too much partying and not enough studying almost got me kicked out of school." She grinned. "I'm trying to reform."

Cate laughed. "Then we're in the same boat. I'm here for the same reason. So, we can go to parties together and keep each other in line. Yes?" She saw Dianna nod. "I've been invited to a party this weekend. It's at Tau Omega Psi. They've invited me to be a little sister. Wanna come along?"

Bingo. Dianna refrained from breaking into a happy dance. *This was way too easy.* Instead, she played dumb. "Tau Omega what? What's that? A fraternity?" She shook her head. "Those guys get pretty wild. I'm not sure—".

Cate popped a waffle into her mouth. "Really? You act like I have no self-control whatsoever. Besides, I'm just checking it out. Not even sure I want to spend any time with those guys. I've only met a few of them. For all I know, the rest of them are a bunch of nerds who do nothing but play video games and expel fumes." She wrinkled her nose. "Like my brothers."

Dianna laughed. *Maybe they're typical college guys or maybe they recruit for a religious cult.* Dianna studied Cate. Hesitantly, she said, "Okay, but we'll be each other's wing person, okay? If some guy gets handsy, the other intervenes. And we need to keep our drinking under control. No waking up in anonymous beds with no memory of how we got there. Been there, done that, done."

Cate pursed her lips, then smiled. "As long as you don't act like the Gestapo or my mother, we're good."

Dianna turned to Hope. "Why don't you show me to my room so I can get settled?" She arched an eyebrow. "And I think you promised me a tour so I can find my classes on Monday. I don't want to be late on my first day. I'm already behind by arriving three weeks after classes have begun."

Cate studied her. "How'd you convince them to let you in so late, anyway?"

"I flunked out at the end of the semester, but my midterms were strong. I managed to convince them that since I'm retaking the classes I flunked, I was already ahead." She grinned. "They bought it." Dianna reached for her bag and motioned to Hope. "Shall we get started?"

Hope smiled. "Yup. Follow me."

Dianna and Hope exited the campus coffee shop and sipped on their pumpkin spiced mocha lattes. They walked to a wooden bench and sat. Dianna smiled at Hope. "So, tell me about Cate. Do you trust her?"

Hope shook her head. "Nope. For all of her declared intentions, she's still a party animal. I went with her to a God's Delight concert and she hooked up with the main preacher, Reverend John. The guy was a stud, but geesh. She came back half-stoned, with no recollection of what happened. She remembers having sex but just doesn't remember with whom. It sounds like the whole thing was an orgy. Lots of drugs and alcohol and free love. She claims something was slipped into her drink, but I think she just may have overindulged. She seems to be a walking, talking example of wretched excess."

Dianna frowned. "Tell me about the concert you went to."

Hope took a long sip of her coffee. "It was total bullshit. The guy kept talking about family and how everyone should work together to do good. They were trying to get people to join them on *their journey.* Unfortunately, no one explained what that journey actually entailed. I think the guy sees himself as some sort of rock star, even if he was kind of old. He kept grabbing a guitar and playing with the band. It was kind of funny, actually." Hope played with her coffee cup. "For a supposed religious cult, there wasn't much talk about

God, which I thought was strange."

"Talking about God too much might be a turn-off. Most people are more interested in what a group like God's Delight can do for them. They want to know the payoff." Dianna set her coffee cup on the bench. "Has Cate had any more contact with them?"

Hope shook her head. "Not that I'm aware of. Of course, I'm not sure she'd tell me if someone had texted or called. I was hoping the last encounter scared the crap out of her. I forced her to go to the student clinic to get checked out because she was complaining about all sorts of aches and pains." She shuddered. "And now she's all excited about this Tau Omega thing. Same bullshit, different group. Claims they only invite the prettiest girls on campus. Sounds like more opportunity for overindulging to me."

Dianna studied Hope. Finally, she said, "Hope, we think they're connected—God's Delight, Tau Omega. Her invite just may be a further attempt at recruitment."

"Oh, Lord. We've got to tell her."

Dianna shook her head. "We can't. It would blow my cover. And Cate doesn't strike me as the type who can keep a secret. We just need to let this play out and see what happens. I will be with her every step of the way. I will do my best to keep her safe, but I need to get her to trust me. If she even suspects I'm not a student, she might out me. I can't take that chance."

"I hate this." Hope narrowed her eyes. "You know it would be smarter to send me in."

Dianna snorted. "Not a chance. You are to be eyes and ears only."

Hope's mouth formed into a pout. "But I'm ready. I know I'm ready."

Dianna sighed. "Not without a law degree. And now that Cade finally finished his, you can't use that against him anymore. Kids are disappearing, Hope. I don't need you to be one of them. Stay out of it. Your time will come." Dianna patted Hope's knee. "When you're ready."

Hope stood and tossed her cup into the receptacle. "So, you'll be tagging along with Cate?"

"She seems to be our best option." Dianna chuckled. "I hope I survive."

"Well, to quote the Greeks at our orientation, *never accept an open cup of anything from anyone and never leave your drink unattended.* Date rape and date rape drugs are a very real thing on campus and there is no better place to strike than at some crazy-ass frat party."

Dianna smiled. "Which is good advice, for a college student. I'll bring my own flavored water. I know better than to drink that piss a frat offers. Hope, do not mess with Cade on this. You won't like the consequences."

"But—"

"Butts are for sitting, girl. Do not mess with Cade. Not only will he see it as a sign of disrespect, but it's also just plain stupid. You could screw up the whole operation."

Dianna surveyed the living room at the fraternity house and held back a smirk. Not much had changed since her college years. The party at Tau Omega Psi was smoky, stinky, and loud.

Already people were fleeing outside to vomit, while still others were passed out on sofas or making out with other partygoers. Those with their wits seemingly intact were either dancing or chatting quietly off to the side. Dianna wasn't sure of the state of those sneaking upstairs, but she hoped they were actually able to consent to whatever activity they engaged in. Morning-afters at a fraternity could be brutal for a woman.

When she and Cate arrived, someone stuck red cups of warm beer into their hands. Dianna found the smell alone repulsive. Cate had downed her beer in one gulp. Then Cate grabbed Dianna's cup and gulped that down as well.

After an unladylike burp, Cate grabbed Dianna's hand. "Let's dance. I'm loving this DJ." She pulled Dianna toward an area cleared for dancing in front of the fireplace. The minute they began to dance, two men appeared at their side, bumping and grinding against them. Dianna gave in to the music but ignored the men. Despite her cover, she was still married, and she absolutely loved her husband. To all other men, she would be an ice princess, with just a promise of melting. She had no intention of crawling into a stranger's lap.

Someone grabbed Dianna around the waist and began to rub against her, their hardness plain. Dianna gently pulled out of their grasp and turned. Anders. She smiled seductively at her husband, ground her body against his, and allowed him to pull her into a kiss. They pretended to be two slightly inebriated strangers doing a little dirty dancing.

When the music slowed, Anders pulled Dianna into his arms, his hands wandering freely. He whispered, "Hi, beautiful. I'm Mark Stiles. What's a beauty like you doing in this shithole?"

Dianna nipped at an ear and replied. "I'm Bennie Marks. And I'm in this shithole hoping to find a rose. You know, the kind that grows out of a pile of manure?"

Anders snorted. His lips moved down her neck and Dianna pulled away, waggling a finger at him. Shouting over the music, she said, "Sorry, sailor, I'm not looking to get laid. I'm just here for the free booze." She giggled and tried to dance away.

Anders pulled her back into her arms and growled into her ear. "I am so not digging all these young pups eyeing my wife. Keep it free and easy, and be careful."

Dianna pushed him away but continued to dance, to all

other eyes, rejecting him. She smiled. "Thanks for the dance, Mark."

Another man joined them and socked Anders on the arm. "Sorry you struck out, old man. How about you sit this one out on the couch, catch your breath? Let the young'uns work their magic."

Anders scowled but turned away. He walked to the bar that had been set up on the side of the room and grabbed the hose attached to the keg to fill a plastic cup.

Dianna watched as the President of the fraternity, Alex Web, tapped him on the shoulder and pointed to different keg across the room.

Anders dumped his beer and walked across the room. He caught Dianna's eye, arched an eyebrow, and nodded toward the keg.

Dianna nodded. *Great, they're doping the women. Let the games begin.*

She glanced around the room, trying to spot Cate. There she was, accepting a drink from the keg Anders had indicated was tainted. Dianna fanned herself and said to the man she was dancing with, "Whew, I'm getting hot. I'm going to get a drink." The man nodded and turned away to dance with another woman.

When Dianna got to Cate, she bumped her with a hip, sloshing the beer from her glass. "Why are you drinking that piss?" she asked, laughing. "They've got the real stuff in the kitchen. Come on."

Cate handed the cup to one of the frat members and followed her.

Dianna grabbed two cups and arched an eyebrow at Cate. "What's your poison?"

"Brandy and coke are fine. You're right about the beer, though. It does taste funny."

Dianna said softly, "I heard one of the guys say that keg is only for the girls. I think it might have something extra in it."

Cate moaned. "Crap, I've only had two beers, but I have no idea where they came from. Maybe we should leave before I—"

Dianna handed her a cup filled with soda and pointed to an empty bottle of brandy. "Looks like someone beat us to the brandy, anyway. Just as well. Let's go get some food."

Cate smiled. "Maybe we should invite some of the guys along? There was one guy I was getting into. But he's the President of the frat." She frowned. "I'm not sure he's into leaving."

Gotta love this girl. She goes right to the top. "Let's go find out." She set her cup down and wrinkled her nose. "Besides, soda without the brandy just isn't the same."

Cate nodded.

CHAPTER FIVE: THE BAIT

Accompanied by three fraternity brothers, including the President, Alex Web, and Cate, Dianna drove to an all-night pizzeria. After Cate complained about feeling off, Dianna had offered to drive her SUV.

Officially, Dianna was a broke college student. She couldn't afford a car.

Cate, on the other hand, wasn't shy about flaunting her wealth. She bragged about family vacations on Martha's Vineyard and Aruba, racing Catamarans on Nantucket Sound, and her family's other holdings.

Dianna suspected Alex was more attracted to her wealth than Cate herself. He was a nice enough guy, but his eyes were calculating. He gave every indication of being a fellow preppy, not immune to the necessity of snagging a wealthy trophy wife and, unfortunately, Cate fit the bill. It probably didn't hurt that Cate was wild and carefree, seemingly up for anything.

One of the other fraternity brothers, Mike Addison, smirked at Cate's flirting and turned to Dianna. "So, Bennie, where do you hail from?"

Dianna smiled. "Actually, I grew up on a farm near Quincy, IL. After my parents died, I saw no reason to stay. My brother took over the farm and I headed to Loyola University in New Orleans. Finished almost three years there, but got into a little academic trouble . . ." She laughed. "So, I came back home. Wisconsin's more affordable. And I missed my brother. He's my only family now. Though with a wife and three kids, I doubt he misses me." She wrinkled her nose and grinned. "Not much a fan of his wife, but my nieces and nephews are adorable." Dianna pulled out her phone and called up a photo. She showed it to Mike. "Gerber babies. Aren't they sweet?"

Cate grabbed her phone and giggled. "God, they all look like you."

Yeah, the Agency is good at hacking family photos. She gazed at Cate. "Better me than her. She's a bit plain." Dianna shifted her attention back to Mike. "So, no, I didn't grow up with fancy vacations and a lot of toys, but I did have loving parents and a comfortable life. I kind of lost my way for a while after they died, but as they say, time heals all wounds. I'm getting there." She smiled sadly. "Someday, I'll get there completely."

Mike frowned. "Gosh, I'm sorry about your parents."

Dianna forced a bitter laugh. "Yeah, it's amazing the damage a drunk five-time DUI offender can do to a Beetle. Forced my parents off a bridge and right into the Mississippi."

Cate gasped. "And here I am bragging about my family and you—"

Dianna waved her off. "You didn't know." Enough deflection. Her real family was alive and well on a farm in Osseo, WI. The fine points of her cover had been heard by the right ears. Dianna had revealed her supposed flaws and her desire for a family connection. The bait was dangled. She just hoped someone from God's Delight would bite. Dianna smiled. "Let's get some pizza. I'm starving!"

Everyone nodded and followed her inside.

After the guys consumed three pizzas and a pitcher of beer, the third fraternity member, Adam Winch, asked, "So, do you girls have any interest in being little sisters? Our house sure could use a little beauty to class up the place."

Cate giggled. "I'm in. All of you are smokin' hot." She nudged Alex. "Especially this one."

Alex smiled and kissed her. "Why, thank you, darling."

Dianna frowned and feigned confusion. "I guess I'm missing something here. What do little sisters do, other than attend parties?"

Mike laughed. "Unfortunately, that's a large part of it."

"What about the little sisters from last year? None of them stuck around?"

Mike shrugged. "Some graduated, others moved on. Being a little sister is hard work. Regardless, having beautiful women around builds our reputation, helps with recruiting."

Dianna studied him, saying nothing.

Alex scowled. "Geesh. Way to be insulting. Little sisters are not whores used to attract and put out for members."

Mike flushed. "I didn't mean . . ."

Alex huffed. "Well, that's the way it came off, man." He gazed at Dianna. "Our little sisters work hard, not for us, but *with* us. And they tend to keep us in line and on task. We do a lot of charity work. We visit the children's hospital during the holidays and distribute toys. We volunteer at a soup kitchen once a month. We participate in fundraisers for various organizations."

Dianna smiled. "Well, that sounds like fun."

Mike nodded. "But our best projects take place out of the country. We work with an orphanage in Bolivia. Last year, we helped install an irrigation system for their community garden. This year, we're going to build a storage shed for supplies and vehicles. With enough volunteers, we might even build an addition onto the main building for the older kids. Give them their own space.

"We work with a group of nuns down there. Pretty cool

group. Some of our members have enjoyed the work so much, they've stayed behind. We're heading out again in two weeks." Mike cocked an eyebrow. "Interested?"

Dianna tried not to show too much interest. "Who are the nuns affiliated with? The Catholic Church?"

Mike shook his head. "No, I get the sense it's nondenominational. But the trip is sponsored by some foundation."

Strange. "Sounds like a good cause, but I'm not sure I can miss school," Dianna said. "I have a tough schedule this year."

"Oh, it's during a class break," Adam said. "Recovery from mid-terms or something. It's a quick in and out."

Dianna shook her head. "I don't even have a passport. I doubt I can get one that quickly. Plus, it's probably not in my budget."

Mike laughed. "No problem. We fly charter. Free. No one even checks for passports. And if they did, we can conjure up a fake in no time."

"Seriously?" *Maybe that's why the students can't be traced. There's no record of who is on the plane.* Dianna smiled. "Can I think about it?"

Mike nodded. "Sure. Just let me know so I can get you a list of what you'll need."

Alex nudged Cate. "How about you, beautiful? Wanna share a sleeping bag with me?"

Cate giggled. "I'm in. Sounds like fun. I'll bring a bikini. Maybe we can find a beach."

Alex smirked. "That's the spirit." He kissed her.

Dianna's mind worked at warp speed. *Is one of these men a recruiter for God's Delight? Or are they just enthusiastic about heading to Latin America for charity work?*

"The Santa Maria Shelter for Children in Bolivia and the GoFlex Foundation. I need you to find out if God's Delight is connected with either of those organizations. This trip may be the funnel." Dianna put her phone on speaker and set it on her bed.

Cade groaned. "God, I hate those ass-wipe Third World countries. They're a great place to hide—people, drugs, arms, dirty money. Even although Bolivia has an extradition treaty with the U.S., they don't honor it. They *refuse* to honor it. That country is so poor, almost anyone or anything can be bought. It's the perfect location for a cult." He sighed. "Any idea where in Bolivia?"

"All I know is they take a private jet to the El Alto International Airport, which I believe is by La Paz," Dianna said. "I checked the God's Delight's website and found nothing. They claim to be headquartered in Maine. There is no mention of outreach to other countries. But the plane is owned by the GoFlex Foundation, so they bear a closer look."

"What about the fraternity? Did you check their website?"

"The local chapter doesn't have a website and the national site mentions trips to Latin America for charitable purposes, but nothing more. And here's the thing—I can't find any little sisters who have made previous trips. Isn't that a little odd?"

"It is," Cade agreed. "So maybe that means only the men return. That they leave the women there. Not sure how could they get away with that, though."

"That's the question, then. Because if they are leaving the women there, they are guilty of kidnapping, trafficking, or worse."

"Remember, there's always a possibility that the women stay voluntarily." Cade was silent for a moment. "Dianna, I need to ask you again. Are you okay with this? This could get ugly."

"Told you, boss. I'm fine."

"Because Janet will kick my ass if this goes sideways and you get hurt."

"She's a fine one to talk," Dianna said. "She's been kidnapped multiple times. Geesh, she should be the one having flashbacks. Not me."

Cade cleared his throat. "But she intended to be taken most of those times. She was bait."

Dianna expelled a frustrated sigh. Softly, she said, "And so am I."

Cade said nothing, then Dianna heard the soft patter of computer keys.

Cade said, "According to Agency maps, Bolivia borders Chile and Peru. Both are really close to the airport. They could easily put everyone on a bus and drive to one of those other countries. And given the lack of border control, no one would even know it."

"So maybe the orphanage isn't really in Bolivia?"

"Or maybe it isn't an orphanage at all. Think about it. Once you get down there and discover there is no children's shelter, how do you get back home? If you can't get on a plane, or even to the airport, you're stuck." He paused. "So, when a benevolent religious commune offers you safe refuge, are you going to turn it down?"

Dianna heard him tap on a few more keys.

"I'll ask Janet to do a little exploring. Maybe we'll find something on their social media accounts or in a satellite sweep."

"Start with the President . . . Alex Web. That guy gives me the creeps and Cate Creighton really has the hots for him."

Cade sighed. "Well, it wouldn't be the first time a man courted a woman for illicit purposes. It's no secret that the Creighton's are powerbrokers and loaded. That's what makes Cate a valuable target."

"Almost makes me wonder why they haven't glommed onto Hope, but then she's not a party girl like Cate."

"Thank God. If she got involved with God's Delight, Mari

and Harun would go ballistic. The Sheikh is overly protective of his daughter. Last year's incident destroyed any illusions he had about his safety in this country. We almost lost our lives when that plane blew up in his neighbor's cornfield, and he brushed it off. But when that terrorist went after Hope at school, he was seriously shaken."

"I'm trying my best to keep Hope out of it, but that kid is sneaky," Dianna said.

"She is, but surely she's no match for you." Cade laughed. "Meanwhile, Janet and I will do some digging. Poke around some more. Express some hesitation about the potential danger. See what they say. Maybe try to get some names of other women who have taken trips.

"If we can't get reasonable answers, both you and Anders will be on that trip, and trust me, it won't be another honeymoon."

The revulsion in his voice put Dianna on high alert.

Chapter Six: The Compound

Dianna and Cate entered the Tau Omega Psi house carrying bags of snacks and food.

Cate had embraced being a little sister with a passion, becoming the party organizer and caterer. These days, she practically lived at the house.

Dianna dumped the bags on a large, long table and turned to Cate. "How do you want to do this?"

"Doesn't really matter. You could dump everything on the floor and these guys would still eat it. They're pigs." She giggled. "Hot sexy pigs, but more bacon than steak."

Dianna's eyes widened. Maybe Cate wasn't so clueless about men after all. Dianna grabbed one of the five-foot subs Cate had purchased. "Well, let's unwrap these and cut them up, and put out plates and napkins. Maybe some of them have evolved just a tiny bit."

Cate laughed. "We can always try." She opened several bags of chips and poured them into bowls they'd bought at a dollar store.

"Maybe we should cut off the kegs a little earlier. Less clean-up. After that last party, this place was disgusting. They should have given us face masks and gloves."

Cate nodded. "And a crate of cleaner, not just a bottle."

A hand crept around Dianna's waist and someone crooned in her ear. "How are you, my lovely?" The man bit her ear.

Slowly, Dianna turned into Anders' arms. "Why Mark," she said sweetly. "It's been awhile. I was hoping I'd see you tonight." She leaned in and whispered into his ear, "I miss you."

Anders pulled back and winked. He said loudly, "Got a room here now. I was kind of hoping I could give you a tour later."

Dianna said loudly, "You wish." She winked. *I'll be there, darling, wet and waiting.*

Alex, the fraternity President walked up behind Anders. "Mark, my man, told you Bennie was a losing proposition. You're just too old for a beauty like her. Maybe you need to aim a little higher, as in age. These young lovelies demand young blood, quality gents, like me." He put his arm around Cate and kissed her. "Right, baby?"

Cate giggled. "I doubt you speak for those two. I've seen them eye-fucking all around campus." She grinned at Dianna. "Time this one got off the celibacy train and kicked it up a notch."

Dianna flushed. "Maybe I'm just picky." She grabbed Anders' hand. "But I would love to see your room."

Anders grinned. "See? Guess this old coot still has it." He kissed Dianna's hand and led her away.

Anders kicked the door to his small room closed and locked it. He grabbed Dianna and pushed her over to the bed. "The walls have ears, so let's make this good."

Dianna moaned as he kissed her neck, then grasped her breasts. She murmured, "I don't give a damn what they hear, dear husband. It's been three long days."

"Careful, Mrs. Mark, I might think you miss me."

Dianna turned and yanked his blue denim shirt from his pants, then unzipped and pulled at his jeans. "I do, dammit. Take it off. Take it all off!"

Anders kicked off his shoes and jeans, and Dianna helped him out of his boxers. He gazed at her and growled. "Now it's your turn."

Dianna lifted her arms as he removed her tee shirt, then she wiggled out of her jeans. Anders unsnapped her bra and tossed it aside. He pushed Dianna onto his single bed and stripped away her panties and socks. Dianna yanked him on top of her and nipped at his shoulder. "God, I missed you."

Anders kissed his way down her body and spread her legs. A raunchy rock song began to play in the living room, the beat thrumming through the thin walls. Anders lapped at Dianna's mons, his fingers separating her lips. His tongue probed inside.

Dianna writhed, grabbing his hair to pull him closer. "My God, Anders. I need you inside me now. Please, baby. Fuck me."

Anders crawled back up Dianna's body and kissed her. "I wish I had my toys with me," he whispered. "I know how much you love those nipple clamps and your butt plug."

Dianna emitted an exasperated sound. She demanded, "Dammit, stop talking and start fucking!"

Anders sighed. "So impatient, wife." He nestled between her legs and stroked her opening with his cock, then thrust inside. Mimicking the rhythm blasting through the walls, Anders thrust harder and deeper.

Dianna bucked against him and screamed, her mind spiraling off into white nothingness. Her body shuddered, then became still. She whimpered. "God, that's how you used to do it when we snuck into the janitor's closet at the law school. Quick and dirty." She sighed. A satisfied smile crossed her face.

Anders slid off her body and pulled Dianna's back to his front. He whispered, "Fraternity guys don't make love — they screw. Best way to build my street cred is to make a beautiful woman scream. Old man, indeed. I am quite sure everyone heard that. I'm going to enjoy your walk of shame, *Bennie*."

Dianna smiled and turned to him, her expression blissful. "As if I could walk. I feel a little like Gumby right now. You might have to carry me downstairs."

Anders kissed her. "Let's take a nap, then head out. By then, everyone will be so drunk, they probably won't notice your debauched state."

Dianna giggled. "Are you kidding? Alex notices everything. I swear he's taking notes."

"Well, if we're lucky, Cate's keeping him occupied."

Cade walked into the Agency's temporary quarters near the UW-Madison campus and nodded at Dianna and Anders. "Well, you were right. God's Delight does have a compound in Latin America, but if we've guessed correctly, it's in Peru, not Bolivia. Still, it's very close to the La Paz airport and the orphanage."

Dianna frowned. "Guessed? You haven't been able to confirm it?"

Cade shook his head. He tapped something on the communications console and a satellite photo of an expansive courtyard surrounded by large buildings popped up onto the white screen. "According to satellite surveillance, there is a possible location in close proximity to the orphanage. Lots of people milling about. But there are also a lot of poppy fields nearby. So, it could be the God's Delight compound, some drug lord's processing plant, or something else. We can't access local property records, and as far as we can tell, there is no signage that indicates ownership or identity.

"While it would make sense to process the poppies and produce heroin on site, it makes just as much sense to locate a religious cult there." Cade pressed a button and more detailed photos of the compound appeared. "We managed to do one fly-by. The place is built like a fortress and guarded, though not as heavily as we would expect a drug cartel's operations to be." Cade tapped another button and a bus painted in a rainbow of colors appeared. "The place is in the middle of the jungle. There is nothing nearby. The only way in and out appears to be on these buses."

Anders pointed at the screen. "Those would be hard to miss."

Cade nodded. "My agents tell me they travel all over that area, including to the orphanage." Cade hit another button on the console and a photo of people in white head-to-toe hooded gowns appeared. "The locals call these people nuns. Apparently, they make the rounds, volunteering at area orphanages and schools, sometimes delivering food to needy families. The buses are used to transport them." He hit another button and the photo of a rough-looking armed man appeared. "Always accompanied by armed muscle, of course."

Dianna cocked an eyebrow. "To protect them or to keep them close?"

Cade shrugged. "Hard to tell. Mostly, however, the locals leave them alone."

Dianna said, "Well, wouldn't that be more consistent with a religious compound? Cartels aren't usually involved in good works."

"Unless the nuns are really mules, used to deliver drugs to the pipeline. Peru, in particular, supplies the European continent. They tend to stay out of American markets. That heroin has to get into the pipeline somehow."

Another photo of the nuns popped up on the screen and Cade highlighted one face. "We attempted to run all of the faces the satellite picked up through our facial recognition programs. Mostly, we couldn't get enough points of recognition. We need eyes with a nose or a mouth, at least. Those damn hoods are great camouflage. We couldn't find Merry

Wright, but this photo gave us pause."

Dianna peered at the photo. She gasped. "Is that—"

Cade nodded. "You tell me. Is that Tillie, the Brit you met in Morocco after being kidnapped by the Vinchenzo Cartel?"

Several years prior, when Dianna was a law student at DeBarkin University outside Milwaukee, she had been snatched by the cartel while jogging. She wound up in Morocco, on sale as a sex slave to the highest bidder. Anders and Cade had rescued her from the auction by posing as buyers. Several Americans had been purchased that day and all were returned safely to the United States. The incident had motivated Dianna to join the Agency. Tillie had been kidnapped off the streets in England and was also up for bid at the auction. They had become friends.

Dianna moved closer to the white screen and studied the photo. She shook her head. "It sure looks like Tillie, but isn't she MISix?"

Cade nodded. An MISix identification card popped up on the screen. "It appears to be the same woman."

Dianna frowned. "But that makes no sense. I thought God's Delight only targeted the U.S."

"Actually, they target people who *live* in the U.S. It appears they don't much care about their nationality or country of origin. There are plenty of Brits, as well as citizens of other countries, who attend colleges in our country. If college campuses are the funnel, it stands to reason that a few foreign students would be swept up as well." Cade paused. "However, Peru also supplies the UK with heroin. Those poppy fields are a bit of a red flag. So, we don't know why she's there. Drugs or missing kids?"

Anders studied the photo. "Why not just ask? We have before."

"I've made inquiries, but no one is confirming or denying." Cade sighed. "However, if she is an agent in place, I'd feel even more comfortable with sending you in. More hands on deck."

"OK, so we still don't know if that's the God's Delight compound, but the orphanage *does* exist?" Anders asked.

Cade tapped on the console and another photo appeared. "This is the Santa Maria Shelter for Children. It's located outside of La Paz, right near the Bolivian-Peruvian border." The single building was constructed of a whitewashed stone. Children were playing right next to it. "As far as we can tell, it is run by nuns from a variety of religious orders. In fact, some appear to be former nuns who simply retained the habit."

"And the Catholic Church permits that?" Dianna frowned. "I would think the church would defrock them or something."

"Except they do good work," Cade said. "They take in children who would otherwise wind up on the streets. Closing the facility down is not worth the PR nightmare. Besides, they are in the middle of nowhere. No one is paying attention to who is actually a member of what order."

Anders studied the white screen. "So, these nuns from Peru also volunteer there?"

Cade punched another button and a new photo revealed several white-cloaked women working with the other nuns at the children's shelter. "Yup. But we don't know why. Think about it. What better place to store or traffic drugs? No one would even look at an orphanage or nuns. It's a brilliant strategy."

Dianna frowned, "So Tau Omega Psi could unknowingly be aiding a drug cartel? That's crazy."

Cade nodded. "Or an unexpected complication."

A confused expression crossed Dianna's face. "We don't know if that's definitely the God's Delight compound, so why are we even going in?"

"Because we need more information, and we can only get that on the ground. Your mission is threefold. One, find out if that compound is indeed run by God's Delight. Two, if it is, determine whether there is a reason for a welfare check on American citizens, in particular, Merry Wright. And three, determine whether Tau Omega Psi is a recruitment funnel for God's Delight and if they are, whether their recruiting is on the up and up. We're looking for any indication of criminal activity." He gazed at Dianna and Anders. "Any questions?"

"How are we supposed to get to the compound?" Dianna asked. "You said it's in the middle of the jungle. It's not like we can order an Uber."

"You are going to have to play it by ear," Cade said. "A lot of the locals use scooters. You may need to borrow one. But the best bet may be to buddy up to the nuns, show interest. If they're recruiting for God's Delight, they'll bite."

Anders asked, "What are our orders if it's a drug cartel?"

Cade snarled. "You cut and run. Do not stick around. Send up the bat signal. Drugs have nothing to do with your mission."

"So, if we discount the drug scenario, this is really a simple in and out." Dianna's eyes narrowed. "No real danger?"

Cade shook his head. "While your assignment may appear to rank low on the danger scale, you really won't know that until you get in there. Stay aware and be wary. Question everything. And be prepared to fail, because frankly, this is a real crap shoot." Cade cocked an eyebrow. "You've had some intense assignments in the past. Lots of guns and glory. This one should barely break a sweat. However, if you do get in trouble, you have the bat signal. Activate it and we'll order an immediate extraction."

Chapter Seven: Bolivia

Anders entered the coffee shop, located several miles off campus, and his gaze swept the customers seated there. He recognized no one.

He turned to Dianna and said softly, "Any idea who we're meeting with?"

"All Cade said is it was someone from the Agency who would provide us with some background on Bolivia. Maybe we're looking for the scholarly type?"

Anders bumped her hip. "Who knows? Let's get some coffee and take a seat. Maybe he or she will find us." He walked to the counter and turned to Dianna. "Carmel Macchiato?"

Dianna nodded.

Anders ordered black coffee for himself and then walked to an empty table, both cups in hand. They sat and sipped, their eyes focused on the entrance.

"Maybe they got held up," Dianna checked her watch. "They're late."

Anders smiled. "No, he just walked in." He waved at a tall, thin man with a full beard. "Harry, over here." The man grinned and mimed getting a coffee.

When he got to their table, Harry pulled a worn messenger bag off of his shoulder and placed it on a chair. Then he man-hugged Anders. "My man, so good to see you."

Anders studied him. Dressed in a pair of torn jeans, a band tee shirt and an Army jacket, Harry looked more like a college student than a covert agent. However, his dark green eyes were wary, darting around the room as if he was expecting trouble.

Harry took off his jacket and sat in the chair opposite Dianna. He nodded at her. "I take it this is the little woman?"

Anders smiled. "Watch it, man. Despite your years with the Seals, she can still kick your ass. But yes." He leaned in and whispered, "Harry, meet Dianna. Dianna, meet Harry."

Harry brushed his long, dark curly hair out of his eyes and grunted.

Anders placed a hand on Dianna's thigh. "He served with me in Afghanistan." He cocked an eyebrow at Harry. "I take it you're here to brief us on Bolivia?"

Harry nodded. A brief smile crossed his face, then he began to speak, softly. "You couldn't have picked a more perfect hellhole. I spent three months there, mostly in a cell, but we won't go there. The place is hardly a tourist's paradise. It has everything—a contaminated water supply, virus-carrying mosquitoes, poisonous snakes, a corrupt government, and all sorts of unpleasant intestinal illnesses and fevers. And it's hot, muggy, and just generally disgusting."

Anders smiled. "And the good news?"

"We can inoculate you against some of the stuff and provide you with pills and medications for some of the other, but never, ever drink anything but bottled water or American sodas in cans. And avoid any type of ice—that's frozen water and it's easy to forget that in the heat—and be careful taking showers.

"The locals are immune to the contamination, so they will insist everything is fine. But they've been drinking that shit all of their lives, so of course, they think their water is clean. It's not. You will get sick and it won't be a twenty-four-hour thing. You can bring Iodine tablets to purify the drinking water, but even that's a risk. There are so many contaminants in the groundwater, God only knows what you're ingesting. The number of pathogens in their water and food is insane."

Harry pulled a sheet of paper from his bag. "I've pulled together a list of what you'll need to take along in a first aid kit, everything from Acetaminophen and Iodine tablets to antibiotics and insect repellant. You need to be cognizant at all times. Only eat food that's been peeled or cooked. Don't play with animals even if they look like pets—some carry rabies or other diseases—and stay the hell away from the snakes. They're nasty suckers and mostly poisonous."

"We'll be near La Paz, so surely they'll have some sort of medical care there," Dianna said.

Harry shook his head. "Those places are far and few between and they require cash payment up front. And if you're American, the price will be especially high." He pulled out another piece of paper and handed it to them. "While the mosquito population near La Paz is not as bad as in other areas of the country, you still need to be careful. Wear lots of *DEET*, bring long pants and long sleeve shirts, sleep under a net, and avoid areas with standing water."

"What about altitude sickness?" Anders asked. "We'll be about four thousand feet above sea level."

"Since you won't be traveling up to higher altitudes, but rather landing in a high-altitude area, your adjustment should be minor. Initially, some shortness of breath or light-headedness, but it should pass quickly. One of the items on your list is Acetazolamide, for altitude sickness. Take it before you land."

Dianna studied the lists. "How do we even get all of this past Customs? This is a lot of stuff."

"Most of it is acceptable. Just make sure you follow TSA rules and you should be okay. And unlike ICE, in Bolivia, a few American dollars supplies a lot of grease. Make a list of everything in your first-aid kit and present it with your passport and a twenty folded inside." Harry pulled another sheet of paper from his bag. "Here's a list of all infectious diseases found in the area. The list is long and rather frightening. Some will require inoculations, others require awareness and vigilance."

Harry took a long sip of his coffee. "The Agency will have an American doctor nearby, probably volunteering at a clinic. You'll get the contact information." He sighed. "Again, stay away from the water and the food, stay out of the hot sun—sun stroke down there, sucks—liberally apply sunscreen and *DEET*, and use your mosquito net, even if you stay someplace without windows. Mosquitos scent new blood and they are good at finding it. Just remember, you're going to a Third World country. They dump raw sewage into their waterways and the streets. Bottled water and antibacterial soap are mandatory. Hell, I wouldn't even swim off their beaches. Those places are worse than public toilets."

Anders groaned. "I feel like I'm going back to Afghanistan."

Harry reached for his jacket and pulled it on. "Trust me, man, this is much worse."

Dianna boarded the private jet and looked around the cabin. There were ten rows of four seats, split into pairs by an aisle. A table and six chairs sat in the back. About half of the seats were filled.

Cate bounced in her seat and called her name. "Bennie! Over here. I saved you a seat." Alex, seated next to Cate, flushed, as if embarrassed.

Dianna studied the other passengers. Adam and Mike were already seated among four new little sisters. And other fraternity brothers were entertaining several more. However, no Anders. *Dammit.* She did not want to be stuck on a long flight next to some horny frat boy. Dianna paused. *Where is he?* They had ridden together to the airport. He should have been right behind her. Dianna began to walk toward Cate slowly.

Just as she reached Cate's seat, Anders rushed into the plane and yelled, "Bennie!" He moved toward her and held up a bag from a famous cookie store. "Sorry I'm late. I stopped to get supplies for the flight." He handed the bag to Dianna and took her duffle bag. Then he whispered, "Had to stop Hope from sneaking onto the plane. She was determined to make the trip and, as she put it, *prove herself.* Thank God Hazelton was right on her tail. I called Cade, then I had to hold Hope until Hazelton caught up." Anders stopped at a row of empty seats and asked loudly, "Window or aisle seat?"

Dianna smiled. Loudly, she said. "Window. I want to see everything. This is my first time out of the country." She slid into the seat, reached for her duffle bag, and slid it under the seat in front of her. One of the most important lessons the Agency had taught her was to always keep her baggage in sight. That prevented *unfriendlies* from removing items while she slept.

Anders took the seat next to her and smiled. He also slid his duffle bag under the seat in front of him and turned to her. He leaned in as if to kiss Dianna and whispered, "Also had to make a last-minute pick-up at the cookie store. Cade is worried we might be doped on the plane." He surreptitiously placed a pill into Dianna's hand. "Drink only from the water bottles we packed and take this before accepting any food." He turned to Cate. "Want a cookie?"

Cate giggled and snuggled into Alex. "No thanks. I think I've got all of the sugar I need."

Dianna groaned. "How many restrooms are there on this plane?"

Alex blinked. "Two. Why?"

Dianna rolled her eyes. "I'm afraid you two are going to do the mile-high thing, leaving the rest of us with bulging bladders."

Cate giggled again. "Now there's an idea." She nudged Alex. "Maybe after dinner, we can indulge in a little dessert."

Anders laughed and leered at Dianna. "How about it, Bennie? Care for a little dessert?"

Dianna opened the bakery bag, removed a cookie, and took a bite. "No thanks. I have all the sugar I need."

Several more people walked onto the plane and took seats. Then a man in a dark blue suit entered. He was older, his graying hair thin. But his eyes were like lasers—sharp and cold. Internally, Dianna shuddered. The man bled malice. He bore watching.

"Okay, folks," the man said. "Before we take off, I'll need all of your passports for the immigration authorities."

Dianna leaned forward in her seat and glared at Alex. "I thought you said we didn't need passports. I don't have one."

Alex held up a bag. "All taken care of." He waved at the man in the suit. "I collected all of them before you boarded, sir. I am sure you'll find everything in order." The man walked over to him and took the bag.

Dianna asked, "Are you with the fraternity?"

The man's mouth twisted into a smile and he snorted. "Not hardly. I'm with GoFlex Foundation. We're paying for your trip." Abruptly, he turned away from her and disappeared into the cockpit. Within minutes, a flight attendant sealed the door and the jet engines came alive. With a light lurch, the plane began to roll down the runway. The flight attendant grabbed a microphone and began reviewing safety measures.

Dianna ignored the woman. Her eyes narrowed. "What was that about?" she whispered.

Anders shrugged. "Maybe they're playing passport roulette. Once you're in a foreign country, a fake passport or no passport can prevent you from leaving and reentering this country. No passport in Bolivia could also land you in jail. The locals probably delight in extracting huge sums of cash before deporting you. They may be trying to keep the passports safe or they could plan to use them to keep us in line."

Dianna's eyes fluttered open when the lights of the plane flashed on.

Anders set down his water bottle and grinned at her. "Hey, sleepyhead. You were out."

Dianna frowned. "What time is it?"

"Just about the dinner hour. Once we eat, it's your turn to stand watch."

"Anything unusual happen?"

Anders leaned in and whispered into her ear. "Alex and some of his buddies have been in and out of the cockpit a few times. Cate joined the mile-high club—I am surprised her screams didn't wake you. Mostly, however, people seem to be drinking a lot and sleeping. However, I can't ID blue suit guy. Alex claims not to know him, says they've never met. I can't decide if he's some sort of thug or actually with the charitable foundation. I sent a photo to Cade. Hopefully, he'll have something soon."

"Did you get a head count?"

Anders nodded. "After we stopped in Dallas, we wound up with twenty men and twelve women." The flight attendant began to make her way down the aisle, dispensing sandwiches, chips, and drinks. Anders pressed another pill into Dianna's hand. "This will keep you awake." He yawned. "God, I really need a nap."

He quickly consumed his sandwich while Dianna watched. She smiled. "You look like such a little boy. Yawning in between wolfing down that sandwich. Get some sleep. I'll keep watch over you."

Anders flushed. "I'm not the one you're supposed to be watching, babe. I'm one of the good guys."

"Don't I know it." She brushed her hand over his crotch. "And there are so many things you're good at."

Anders snorted and pushed his seat back. He closed his eyes and quickly fell asleep.

Dianna studied the other passengers. Most everyone was pushing their seats back and closing their eyes. Her attention shifted to the cockpit as Alex and the man in the blue suit walked out, obviously in deep conversation. They appeared to be arguing. The man scowled at him and held up five fingers, mouthing the words, "Pick five." Dianna slitted her eyes partially closed and watched as the man pointed at four women, including Cate. Then he pointed at her. *Alright then, I'm one of five, but five what? What exactly do they intend to do with us?*

Alex huffed and walked away from the man. With an exasperated sigh, he sat down and nuzzled the neck of a sleeping Cate. Then he wrapped his arm around her and pulled her head onto his shoulder.

Dianna hid her frown. Maybe Alex wasn't as calculating as he appeared. If he truly cared about Cate, it might be to his benefit to keep her safe. *Interesting.*

Cade Matthews entered the unmarked conference room at Mitchell International Airport and flashed a badge at the official. "I'll take it from here. Thanks." The woman nodded and left the room.

He sat at the small table and glared at Hope. Her eyes grew wide, but she said nothing. Cade remained silent, holding her gaze, his anger apparent.

Hope shifted uncomfortably. She picked at a cuticle on her right thumb and peeked up at him through her thick black bangs. Finally, she said softly. "I only wanted to help."

Cade scowled. "You almost blew the entire operation. What the hell were you thinking, Hope? What would you have done if you had been caught entering Bolivia illegally?"

"Well, Anders and Dianna were there. And my roommate, Cate."

"And none of them could have helped you. Anders and Dianna are undercover. Cate has no political sway, her mother does. You could have been left to rot in prison. If someone managed to get word to your parents, you'd be endangering them as well as our mission. Again Hope, what the hell were you thinking?"

A sheepish expression crossed Hope's face. "I thought if I showed you that I can handle myself in difficult situations, you'd fast track me into the Agency."

Cade emitted an exasperated sigh. "All you did was prove you're not mature enough to work for me. What you did was impulsive and reckless. Anders was forced to put his cover at risk to contain you." He shook his head. "You put your selfish needs over everyone else's. Why the hell would I want someone like that at my Agency? My agents need to have each other's backs. They risk their lives daily. They need to know that they can trust their partners to protect their covers and their mission."

Hope fought back tears. She said softly. "I'm sorry."

"Wow! You think that will suffice if you blew Anders' cover? What if he gets killed because of your recklessness? What will you do then? Do you think Dianna will accept your apology?" Cade leaned forward, his eyes hard. "If you ever pull a stunt like this again, I will personally see to it that you never receive security clearance for any work with the

U.S. Government. And without that clearance, there is no governmental agency that will recruit or accept you."

Hope gasped. "You wouldn't . . ."

Cade cocked an eyebrow. "Yes, I would. All you've proven today is that you aren't ready, Hope. Clearly, you have some growing up to do. Perhaps you should try to do it in law school. You may be smart as a whip, but it's book smarts, not street smarts. I need my agents to have both."

A single tear dripped down Hope's cheek and she swiped at it. "You're going to tell my parents, aren't you? Oh God, they're going to make me come home and go to some online college." She sobbed. "I totally blew it. I didn't think — "

"Exactly, you didn't think. You need to grow up and learn how to think before you act. In my line of work, impulsiveness is a death sentence. You blew it, Hope. Big time. I'm not going to tell your parents. That's on you, but know that I was considering admitting you into a training program while you completed your law degree. I can see now that would have been a mistake." His hard gaze settled on Hope. "You simply aren't ready." He pushed back from the conference table and stood up. "Come on. Hazelton is waiting outside, and he is royally pissed. I suspect it is going to take some time before he trusts you again." He started walking toward the door, then stopped. "Can't say I blame him. I'm afraid it's going to be a while before a lot of people trust you. You really blew it, squirt."

The private jet landed roughly at the El Alto International Airport in La Paz. As the passengers rose out of their seats and began collecting their baggage, the hatch was opened and two uniformed officials entered.

Dianna watched carefully as the man in the navy-blue suit handed one of the officials a thick envelope. The customs agent stuffed it into what looked like a messenger bag, then removed a stack of yellow cards.

After the officials left the plane, the man turned. "Okay, everyone, gather your belongings. Make sure you get a visa when you leave the plane and keep it on your person at all times. Do not surrender it to anyone. Then head to one of the buses located beside the plane and we'll be on our way."

Dianna muttered to Anders. "Is he protecting us or leading us like lambs to the slaughter?"

Anders leaned in and nuzzled her neck, then whispered, "Cade hasn't gotten back to me yet. Mike seems to know him and some of the other guys are at least comfortable with him, so while he may not be one of the good guys, he is known." He pulled her from her seat and grabbed her hand. Loudly, he said, "Come on sleepy head. We got here just in time to head to bed."

Playing along, Dianna groaned loudly. "I hope there's a beach. Do you think there's a beach? I know we're here to work, but I would sure like to get a little sun while we're here."

Cate giggled and turned to her. "I'm with you there, Bennie. A little beach time seems like a fair trade-off for volunteering our time."

Alex grabbed Cate by the hips and pulled her against him. "There's a topless beach a few kilometers from the orphanage. I checked." He kissed the top of her head. "Now that's a perfect reward for working our asses off."

Cate wiggled her hips, rubbing against him. "So glad you think so."

Alex gently pushed her into the aisle, guiding her to the door of the plane. "Let's get moving, then."

Anders and Dianna followed him out of the plane. It was already evening, but the sun was still bright. Dianna shielded her eyes and gazed around the private charter airstrip.

Her focus landed on the waiting buses. They were the same ones she had seen in the photos. Brightly colored, like the old flower power Volkswagen vans of the 60's. *Interesting.*

Anders studied the buses. "Maybe this is the only reliable transportation in the area," he said softly. "Let's see how this plays out."

As they approached the buses, two women dressed in white robes, their heads covered with matching hoods, stepped off one vehicle and stood by the door. Silently, they directed the men to one bus and the women to the other. Anders led Dianna to a bus and attempted to board with her.

Alex walked up behind them and cleared his throat. "These are loaned buses. The people who own them agreed to transport us to the orphanage. But apparently, they don't believe in mixing the sexes. Sorry man, you need to join the other men, or we'll be walking. It's not like we have a choice."

Anders shrugged. "Yeah, okay. When in Rome . . ."

His eyebrows lifted and he nodded at Dianna. Quickly, he touched his hand to his heart. Their private signal. *Be safe.*

CHAPTER EIGHT: DIVERSION

Dianna's face was glued to a window as the buses pulled into the courtyard of the Santa Maria Shelter for Children, a sprawling one-story building constructed of what looked like white-washed adobe.

The courtyard was empty, but a few chickens were wandering about in the waning light, squawking and batting their wings as they chased each other.

Cate pushed her aside and stared out the window. "I figured it would be primitive, but this place is like something out of an old western. I wonder if they even have running water." Cate narrowed her eyes. "Are those . . . chickens?"

Dianna laughed. "Dorothy, you're not in Manhattan anymore. Those chickens are probably their next meal."

Cate threw herself back against the hard bench seat. "I can do this," she muttered. "My nails will go to shit and my pedicure is doomed and I'll probably itch like I have fleas, but it's only for a week. I can handle this."

Dianna patted her leg. "You'll do fine, darling. Just make sure you stay with the group and don't wander off."

The bus came to a stop. One of the nuns seated at the front of the bus stood and gestured toward the female passengers, indicating that they should follow her. She led them to the back of the building and pointed at two other structures. She led the women to one. The men were led by the other nun to the other.

Cate said, "Guess we're not camping out under the stars, anyway. Those look like dormitories."

Dianna followed Cate into the first building. There was a gathering room off of the entrance, but the nun led them down a narrow hallway, past many closed doors. Finally, the nun began opening doors and pointed to the twelve women individually, indicating which should enter.

At the end of the hallway, the nun stopped and indicated that the remaining five women should follow her. Dianna gazed at Cate, her eyebrows raised in question. They were the five women pointed out by the man in the blue suit. She tried not to frown.

Cate grinned. "Maybe we get to bunk with the boys?"

Dianna laughed. "Or maybe we *do* have to sleep in a tent."

The nun led them out of the building and back to a bus. She indicated that the five women should board.

Cate stopped short. "What are they doing?"

Dianna stepped in front of the other girls and asked the nun, "Where are you taking us? Why can't we stay with the others?"

The women pulled out a small notebook and began to write. Then she ripped out the page and handed it to Dianna. It read: *Dorms are full. We are taking you to our compound. Much better accommodations.*

Dianna frowned. "Why can't we double up? Or maybe stay in that big hall? We don't want to be separated from our group." She showed the note to Cate. "We need to tell the others."

The nun handed Dianna the notebook and pen, indicating that she should write. Dianna shook her head. *No dice, lady. No way am I going anywhere without speaking to Anders.* She held up a finger. "One minute. I want to speak to the men."

Dianna walked into the men' dormitory and called out for Alex. When he, Mike, and Anders appeared, she said, "They want to move a few of us someplace else, the nun's house or compound or something. They say there's not enough room.

I don't think that's a good idea."

Mike shrugged. "Oh, it's nothing. That happened a few trips back. The girls actually liked staying there. You'll be returned in the morning to work with us. No one has ever complained. In fact, they rave about the amenities at the nun's compound. Better rooms, a hot spring, good food. You'll be brought back here every day."

Alex frowned. "This is my first trip down here, but I've heard a lot about the other trips. I've never heard any complaints. It sounds like a logistical problem. I know we overbooked. I just thought we'd double up or something, but the rooms are seriously small. We'd have to sleep on top of one another. Frankly, I consider this a bonus."

Mike nodded. "Yeah, what woman doesn't love hot springs and a decent bed? We guys will rough it. We're tough."

Dianna studied Mike. He clearly had no concerns, but then he didn't have a girlfriend being shipped off to the unknown. "Have you been to this compound? Do you know where it is? Who runs it?"

Mike said, "The nuns. But as I said, we saw the girls every day when they came back to work. Some of them said it made the whole trip bearable. Look, just try it. If you're still uncomfortable tomorrow, we'll try to figure something else out."

Dianna nodded. Every instinct was on high alert. Yet she had a job to do, and if this led her to God's Delight, she couldn't pass up the opportunity. She gazed at Anders. "Well, if you guys say it's okay, I'm going to trust you. I guess we'll see you tomorrow."

As she turned to walk away, Anders again touched his hand to his heart. *Be safe.*

Dianna and Cate boarded the bus and the driver steered it off the grounds onto a dirt road. The road had obviously been rough cut through the jungle and was just wide enough for one vehicle. As they traveled away from the orphanage, branches and leaves slapped against the windows. Dianna found the sound unsettling. Her stomach was already churning. *God, I hate not knowing where we're headed.*

She brought her focus back to the bus and the route they were traveling. They appeared to be moving deeper and deeper into the jungle. She saw no other road nor any buildings. No other vehicles. Not even a sign that they were crossing into another country. The jungle was thick, the cawing of birds and the squeaks of what she assumed were monkeys occasionally breaking the silence. Soon, the bus pulled up to a high stone wall with a large wooden gate.

Dianna fought back a sudden rush of panic. *Where did that come from?* She brushed at the sweat that was forming on her forehead. Unbidden and unwelcome memories began to spiral through her mind. *High stone walls. An imposing mansion. The genie-infused voice of a malevolent slave trader. Women bound, some gagged, as they were led into large cages in a basement. Desperate women, afraid . . .*

Cate grabbed her hand, forcing Dianna back to the present. "Wow. You just got really pale. You okay?"

Dianna took a deep breath and tried to smile. "Sorry, I think the heat or the altitude is getting to me." *Buck up, Dianna. You have a job to do.* Dianna reached into her bag and removed a bottle of water. She unscrewed the cap and although it was warm, drank deeply.

The gate was opened and the bus moved into a courtyard. The layout was the same as that depicted in the satellite photos Cade had shown them. There were five buildings in the compound. One was a large mansion of three stories, with many, many windows. Another was only one story, with a few windows on the first floor, a playground off to the side. Several other buildings were two stories high, with windows at set intervals. The courtyard was dimly lit and no one was about. Clearly, everyone had settled in for the night. Her gaze swept the buildings again, looking for some sort of signage, but she saw nothing. The bus moved slowly through the compound and stopped at one of the two-story buildings.

The nun stood and indicated that the women should follow. She led them into the building and down a long hallway. One by one, each woman was shown into a room. When they got to end of the hallway, the nun pointed to Cate and gestured to one room. Then she pointed at Dianna and gestured to the other.

None of the other women appeared concerned about the arrangement, so Dianna turned and walked into her room. It resembled a college dormitory. There was a built-in dresser and desk, as well as a small closet. In the corner was what appeared to be another closet. Dianna walked to it and opened the door. Inside was a small toilet, a shower, and some towels.

Her eyes turned to the twin bed set slightly off center in the room. The regular size mattress bore white sheets, a pillow, and a blue blanket. It was also covered by a mosquito net. Dianna frowned. It was hardly luxurious, but it was better than she had expected.

Dianna checked her watch. They had set their clocks ahead to sync with local time. It was almost midnight. *Guess it's time for bed.* Dianna set her duffle bag on the desk and began to unpack. She placed her clothing in the dresser, her toiletries in the bathroom, a reading tablet on her bed, and the semi-empty duffel bag in the closet.

After ensuring the door to her room was locked, Dianna headed to the bathroom. She removed her clothing and pulled a disposable wet bath sheet from a plastic container. She used it to scrub her body. Dianna poured bottled water onto a washcloth to wipe her face and then brushed her teeth.

After she donned a tank top and pajama shorts, she moved to the bed. Dianna pulled up the netting and settled under a sheet and blanket. The room was clearly temperature controlled. In fact, it was a bit chilly. She rolled onto her side and turned on the reader. As if on cue, the single fluorescent tube that ran the length of the room dimmed, emitting only a soft blue glow. *Hmmmm.* A few minutes later, a soft whir, similar to white noise, filled the room. *Double Hmmmm.*

She squinted to read in the odd light. After a few minutes, Dianna gave up and closed her eyes. She slept.

They were chanting. The voices were low and dim at first but slowly increased in volume until her walls shook with it. Dianna clapped her hands over her ears and groaned. "OMG, shut up!"

She threw off her covers and sat up. Slowly, Dianna removed one hand and tried to focus on the words. "God's vessel . . . serve . . .adoration" She frowned and removed the other hand from the other ear. Again, she tried to hear the words. "He is God's vessel. Our leader into the divine light. We shall serve and prostrate ourselves before him. Our adoration is to God's delight." Was that supposed to be a prayer?

Suddenly, there was silence. Dianna waited. More silence. Dianna laid back onto the bed and pulled up her covers. Just as she was drifting off, the chant began again, this time at a lower volume. Dianna found herself straining to listen. She sat up and yelled, "Dammit!" She stood up and marched to her door, opened it and peered into the hallway. The hallway was dark, but hooded figures in white were moving past her, each holding a small candle, softly chanting. When she attempted to step out further into the hallway, an armed guard appeared at her side. "This is their time of worship," he whispered in a thick Spanish accent. "Please don't disturb them. Go back to your room."

Dianna nodded, stepped back, and closed her door. Her sleep-

addled brain slowly began to decipher what she had seen. Chanting nuns. Praise to someone. She strained, trying to hear the diminishing chant. But she couldn't stay awake. So sleepy. So very sleepy.

The next morning, the sun streamed in through the window, waking Dianna from a troubled sleep. Her blanket had been tossed aside and her reader was on the floor. She sat up and walked to the closet, opened her bag and withdrew clean clothing.

She again cleansed her skin with one of the body wipes and combed a dry shampoo through her hair. Dianna wasn't ready to risk a shower. After dressing and spraying *DEET* over her clothing and any exposed skin, she pulled a sun hat onto her head. Quickly, she stuffed her Visa, money, phone, identification, some miniature trackers, and tool kit into a money belt and attached it around her waist, pulling her shirt over it. *No sense in leaving anything behind.* This wasn't a hotel. There was no guarantee someone wouldn't be searching her room, especially since the doors only locked on the inside.

Finally, Dianna pulled on a pair of sunglasses, walked to Cate's room, and knocked on the door. No response. She knocked again.

"There you are," Cate said, walking down the hallway toward her. "I was getting worried. The other girls came and got me for breakfast. When we knocked at your door, no one answered. We figured you were in the shower. You almost missed it and it was fabulous." She yawned. "I slept like a baby. How about you?"

"I slept like shit. Strange dreams all night long."

Cate laughed. "Kind of why I took a sleeping pill. I can never sleep in new places."

"I was a little freaked out with that strange blue light and the wind machine. Then I thought I heard people chanting."

Cate frowned. "What blue light? What wind machine?"

"Come on, I'll show you." Dianna walked back into her room and flipped on the light switch. A soft white light glowed from the fixture. *WTF?* She turned to Cate. "I swear, it was blue. All night long." She listened. The white noise that had bothered her was also gone.

Cate shrugged. "You must have been dreaming. Sometimes dreams feel so real, it's hard to tell when they're not." She tugged at Dianna's hand. "Let's get you some breakfast. Their mango pancakes are amazing. Maybe you'll feel better after you've eaten."

Dianna followed Cate to a dining hall. It was filled with people. Nuns. Other men and women. Children. People moved around gracefully, all with peaceful expressions on their faces. They spoke quietly, if at all.

While some people nodded at Dianna or Cate, few looked at them directly. Most were indistinguishable with their hoods. No one attempted to engage them in conversation. *Strange. You'd think they'd be curious about newcomers.* Dianna tried to catch a few faces, but without seeing hair and eyes, there was no way she could match them to any of the photos she had been shown. Merry Knight should have been noticeable simply by virtue of her long, curly black hair and striking blue-grey eyes, but in a crowd of white hoods, Dianna was unable to identify her.

Cate led her to a self-serve area where a variety of breakfast foods lined glass shelves and then to a counter where a hoodless man stood flipping pancakes. "Hey, Fred," Cate said cheerfully. "Hook my friend up with some pancakes, please."

He nodded and piled a plate high with thick, large discs, handed it to Dianna, and winked. *Finally, a full face.* Unfortunately, not one she recognized.

Dianna smiled at him and took the plate. Then she grabbed a bottle of juice, comforted by the fact that the plastic seal around the screw top was still intact. She had taken a pill to counteract any pathogens that might cause intentional problems, so she dug into the food. Despite the fact that she felt sluggish, Dianna she was hungry.

After her stomach was full, she sighed. Maybe all she had needed was a good meal. She stood and walked to a tray set off to the side and deposited her plate and utensils there. She turned to Cate. "Let's go find out how we're supposed to get back to the orphanage. We have a busy day ahead."

CHAPTER NINE: DELUSIONS

Anders hoisted the frame he and a few others had constructed out of rough-cut beams and, with Dianna's help, carried it to the site of the shed.

Since the shed would have a dirt floor, trenches had been dug to hold the frames in place. Once the walls were lowered into the narrow openings, other volunteers filled the trenches with dirt to hold the frames in place. Then they nailed the corners of the frames together to keep them upright.

"Are you sure you weren't dreaming?" Anders asked Dianna. "Cate says she didn't see or hear anything and none of the other girls have mentioned anything either. Why would they single you out?"

"I can't explain it. There was a blue light. It made reading difficult. I know I didn't imagine it. And that hissing noise was just weird."

Anders frowned. "Maybe you're just looking for things that aren't there. Did you see anything that confirmed the compound was run by God's Delight?"

Dianna shook her head. "Nothing. And I think if there was, Cate would have noticed. She is not fond of those people. And now she seems happy as a clam." She frowned. "There are some armed guards, though. As we left this morning, I spotted some walking around the compound."

Anders studied her. "How many? Enough to keep people safe from intruders or enough to launch a full out battle if attacked?"

"Only a few. Two roaming the grounds. Four at the front gate."

"Well, that makes sense. They are in the middle of the jungle."

"The place looks like a small town, really. A lot of money has been invested there. I haven't had a chance to look around, but it doesn't give off a cartel vibe. There's no sense of fear." A puzzled look crossed Dianna's face. "But something's off. I just can't quite put my finger on it." She leaned into Anders. "I've had a few panic attacks, too. I've never had those before. Not even when I was kidnapped. So why now? What's triggering those?"

Anders chewed on his bottom lip. "Maybe a subconscious fear that you'll be trapped or held against your will?" He studied her. "Panic attacks could put you off your game. I need you one hundred percent. Say the word and I'll pull you."

Dianna glared at Anders. "Don't you dare. If I need to be pulled off this mission, that will be my decision."

"No, babe. I'm your superior. It will be my decision and only mine." Anders turned from her and swiped at his forehead, then wiped his hands on his shorts. Loudly, he said, "My God, I don't mind the heat, but the humidity here is stifling. I feel like a wet noodle."

Alex laughed and dropped some wood by Anders' feet. "We'll probably sweat off ten pounds before the week is over." Alex winked at Dianna. "I'm sure you ladies will love that."

Dianna smirked. "Way to be a pig, Alex. I admit I wasn't prepared for the humidity. I feel gross. But I prefer to lose my weight in other ways." She winked back at him. "Maybe Anders and I will join the mile-high club on the way home. I call first dibs on one of the plane's bathrooms. You and Cate will have to wait."

Anders grabbed Dianna's hand and walked over to the water station Cate had set up. She sat on a chair, shaded by a tree, reading a book. When they approached, she reached into a cooler and handed them each a bottle of water.

Dianna arched an eyebrow. "Enjoying your vacation, Cate?"

Cate blushed. "Hey, Alex said I wasn't needed on the work crew, that I was better off protecting the water supply. If we run out, we'll be in trouble. It's not like I have the means to boil local water. As it is, I may have to head into town for more bottles. We're running low."

"That's not a great idea, Cate. You've heard all of the stories about Americans being attacked or kidnapped around here. It isn't safe." Dianna leaned against the tree and pulled her hair off of her neck. It was wet and unwieldy. She studied Cate. "Make sure you stick with the group at all times. Especially after dark."

"Bennie, stop being an old mother hen. I'll be fine. It's not like I can go clubbing around here."

Anders snorted. "Thank God for small favors. I imagine a bunch of American college students whooping it up in a club, drunk on their asses, would be easy pickings."

Dianna entered her room and quickly sat on her bed. She didn't feel well. She didn't have a headache exactly, just a poke of pain here and there. And while her stomach turned uneasily, it wasn't enough to send her running to a restroom—just enough make her feel like she was coming down with something. And although she wasn't sweating, she felt hot. Real hot. As if her body was burning from within. What the hell was going on?

She had been careful to drink only bottled drinks and had taken the Agency-prescribed pill to combat any pathogens in the food. Maybe she was having an allergic reaction to something else. But what?

A brisk knock on the door brought Dianna to her feet. "Dianna? Are you okay?" *Cate*. Dianna opened her door and peered out. Cate stood there with a nun hovering behind her. "Not really," Dianna responded. "I just want to lay down and get some sleep."

"Well, I have a better solution. There's a communal bath here for the women. It's fed from a local spring and the locals believe it has healing properties. Why don't we give it a try?" Cate arched an eyebrow. "You've been spraying insect repellant pretty heavily and that stuff can make you sick. One of the nuns gave me something that is supposed to be better for long-term application, but you have to apply it to clean skin. I figure a hot spring has to be better than the showers here. Why don't we try it? And then tomorrow, let's switch your bug spray to something else."

Dianna sighed. At this point, she'd try anything. She couldn't afford to be sick. Dianna changed out of her clothing into a bathing suit, then donned a robe provided by the nun. They were led to a dimly lit room with a large pool at the center. Steam rose from the water, shadowing the occupants. All Dianna could see was a lot of faceless heads. She wasn't even sure whether they were women. *Thank God, I wore a bathing suit.* She and Cate removed their robes and entered the pool. The water was hot and soothing.

They sat at the edge of the pool, away from others in the spa. Dianna tilted her head back, closing her eyes. She sighed. "God, I feel better already."

Cate laughed. "Bet you anything it was the *DEET*. I don't know what's in the spray that the nuns gave me, but it must be working. I feel great and, look, not a single bite." She languidly lifted an arm.

Dianna tried not to frown. Cate seemed awfully relaxed.

And since when did bug spray make anyone feel great? Usually, it was sticky and smelly and . . . Dianna studied Cate. She did seem awfully happy. *After a day in the heat and humidity, you'd think she'd be as cranky as I feel.*

"Bennie, look over there." Cate nodded her head to the opposite side of the pool. "All those women are bald! I thought I was seeing things with the mist and all. But damn, they're all bald."

Dianna peered across the room. The women were congregated at the other side of the pool. As they romped and played with each other in the water, their scalps gleamed. Nude, they also appeared to have no body hair. *Damn, they're indistinguishable. How am I supposed to identify anyone?* "Maybe it's easier to deal with the heat or the bugs?"

Cate shook her head. "Maybe, but without hair, they all look alike." She giggled. "Like a bunch of aliens."

Dianna shifted uneasily. She knew from Catholic grade school that nuns embraced uniformity as a way to rid themselves of the sins of vanity or jealousy. However, it was also a way to strip people of their individuality and identity, something cults often did. "That's kind of creepy." Dianna felt the air shift and looked to the doorway. Six women entered, all with long flowing hair. She frowned. "Except . . ."

"Wonder who those babes are," Cate whispered. Then she frowned. "Wait a minute. I know that woman."

"What?"

"That's Sister Bethany. Reverend John's wife." Cate sunk lower into the pool. "Shit. Does this place belong to God's Delight? Dammit, I should have known he'd find some way to get me down here." Cate ducked behind Dianna.

"Wait a minute. What are you talking about?"

Cate sighed. "I hooked up with Reverend John when he was in Madison. He kept calling, but I blocked his number."

Dianna frowned. "You sure this isn't just a coincidence?"

Cate shuddered. "Not likely. That guy was all over me.

Totally freaked me out. He started texting me. Calling and leaving messages. Invited me on the road with him. Talked about how good we'd be together. Kept inviting me to join him in South America." She groaned. "I didn't know he was married until after I met her. This is so uncool. I had no intention of seeing him again. Dammit. I should have stayed home."

Dianna watched as the women discarded their robes and moved toward the water. "I think they're coming over here. Put your game face on. Let's hear what they have to say." The women entered the pool and swam en masse to Cate and Dianna. Bethany, a tall, well-endowed brunette stood. She swept her long hair over a shoulder, revealing her naked upper body, and smiled. "Cate, right? I remember you from our stop in Madison. I'm so glad you could make the trip."

Dianna studied the woman. She looked every inch the classic, snooty debutante. How did someone like her wind up married to the leader of a cult?

Cate appeared alarmed. "You knew I was coming?"

Bethany shrugged. "We take a special interest in the children's shelter. We're aware of everything that happens there. We often work with the volunteers. I saw your name on the list for the group from Madison." She nonchalantly swirled some water with her hand. "You will appreciate the accommodations here." Bethany curled her lip up in disgust. "The rooms at the orphanage there are rather primitive." She smiled politely at Cate. "Perhaps we can catch up later?"

Cate opened her mouth to respond, but the woman cut her off. She stuck her hand out to Dianna. "Hi, I'm Bethany." She gestured to the other women. "We are *The Chosen*. We assist Reverend John in his international ministry." She smiled proudly. "I am also his wife."

Dianna took her hand and shook it. "Bennie. Cate and I are roommates in Madison."

A sly look entered Bethany's eyes. "Oh, I see."

Dianna asked, "So, this compound is owned by God's Delight?"

Bethany nodded. "Yes, our own heaven on Earth. A place to embrace the teachings of Reverend John and follow him to a better, more satisfying life. We have a very solid community here."

Dianna studied her. "Well, I'm sure we'll be comfortable enough for the week."

Bethany smiled and swam away. The other women followed her.

Dianna studied their faces, but no one matched the photo of Merry Wright. However, one woman did stand out. *Tillie.* How had she managed to become a member of The Chosen? And was she undercover or a convert?

Tillie barely glanced at her, her expression guarded. Then she swam to the others.

CHAPTER TEN: THE CHOSEN

A loud knock at her door jolted her awake. Dianna moaned. She had slept like a rock and her eyelids felt gritty. *What the heck?* She sat up, pushed aside the mosquito net, and stood. She walked to the door and opened it. *Tillie.* "Yes?"

Tillie smiled. In a crisp British accent, she inquired, "Did you sleep well?"

Dianna rubbed her eyes. "I guess."

"The springs that feed our baths are quite special. *Very* calming."

Dianna studied her. "Apparently. I was out like a light."

Tillie nodded. "The springs affect everyone that way." She paused. "I've come to accompany you to breakfast. My sisters tell me no one has shown you around the compound. I imagine you desire a tour?"

"Sure, but they're expecting us at the orphanage . . ."

"Oh, we've informed them that you won't be coming to-day. Our buses are having mechanical difficulties." She shot Dianna a carefree grin. "The jungle air messes with the mo-tors of the buses sometimes. Might as well take advantage of the situation and show you around our amazing compound.

"You may find it so enticing that you'll want to stay."

What the fuck? Dianna looked directly into Tillie's eyes. Her gaze was steady. "What about the other girls?"

"Oh, they've already started their tours. You'll probably see them at dinner."

Dianna glanced down at her nightgown. "I'll need to

change . . ."

Tillie nodded. "Of course. May I suggest one of the habits the nuns wear? Those are made of special material. Not only do they block out the rays of the sun, they effectively wick sweat, keeping you cool. And best of all, the fabric repels mosquitos."

Of course, they do. Dianna pretended to frown. "But I don't have a habit. All I have are khakis and long sleeve shirts."

Tillie *tsked.* "Those will just make you hot. Check the bottom drawer of your bureau. One should have been placed there before your arrival."

Okay, she wants me in the nun's habit. Why? What's next? Shave my hair?

A strange look entered Tillie's eyes. "Really," she said, her voice almost pleading. "You'll be more comfortable while we explore the grounds."

Slowly, Dianna nodded. "Give me a few minutes." She began to close the door.

Tillie stuck her foot in the way. "If you don't mind, I'll just wait on your bed. We can chat while you get ready. I can answer any questions you might have." Tillie walked to the dresser, opened the bottom drawer, and pulled out a habit. She handed it to Dianna and smiled. "You really will love it. It's so much more comfortable than street clothes."

Dianna took the habit and headed to the bathroom, closing the door halfway. She didn't want Tillie to see that she was wearing her money belt, with all of her tools, under her nightgown. Dianna didn't yet know if Tillie was friend or foe. And she wasn't about to ask. "So, how long have you lived here?" Dianna asked.

"About six months. I joined at the invitation of Reverend John. I met him and was simply blown away by his view of the world. It just made so much sense."

"How did you meet Reverend John?"

"Oh, at a party in New York City. A friend invited me. It's

was a fundraiser for God's Delight. Lots of big money. He is quite compelling, and the donors love him."

Now that's interesting. Dianna adjusted her travel wallet, ensuring her tools—lock picks, weapons, explosive charges, trackers and bugs, and defense spray—were in place. While the bat signal had been implanted in one back molar and an anti-doping solution in another, those were only for true emergencies. The habit would hide her belt perfectly. "Were you in New York for work or play?"

Tillie laughed. "Not working, simply playing."

"Still, you must have left a lot behind to move all the way to South America. It is quite a change from New York or even London. That took guts."

Tillie tittered. "You don't know Reverend John. He can be *quite* persuasive."

Wait, what? Dianna withdrew into the recesses of the bathroom and removed her pajamas. She wet a washcloth with a fresh bottle of water and washed her face, then she brushed her teeth, rinsing with the remaining water in the bottle. She slipped on underwear and the habit, then exited. "What's so special about Reverend John?"

"We believe he is the Living Christ. It is an honor to serve him. He has changed my life. He has changed many lives." Tillie stood and handed her a pair of sandals.

Dianna paused. *Does that mean she's having sex with him?* Dianna sat on the bed and strapped them on. "Are you sure I don't need any bug spray? I feel pretty exposed."

Tillie shook her head. "They spray the compound daily, and the fabric of your habit really does deter airborne pests. Living down here has its deficits, but all are manageable." Tillie walked to the doorway, opened the door, and said formally, "Come, I want to show you my wonderful world."

Tillie led Dianna out into the stone-paved courtyard. Brightly-colored flower gardens were scattered about. Nuns knelt in some of the gardens, planting, pruning, or weeding. Several nodded to Tillie as they passed. "This is our version of paradise," Tillie said as she walked. "We've been encouraged to bring forth the beauty from our lives and give them a place here. These gardens represent the splendor of God's gifts, the magnificence of nature."

"There seems to be a lot of nuns around. Are they responsible for maintaining the compound?"

Tillie nodded. "We serve at the pleasure of Reverend John. The nuns are dedicated to providing him with an environment filled with beauty and plenty."

"Plenty?" Dianna cocked her head. "As in money?"

Again, Tillie smiled. "As in cultivating God's bounty."

Dianna let her confusion show. "I don't understand."

"Come, let me show you." Tillie walked behind the mansion that Dianna assumed was Reverend John's home. A large field filled with plantings extended to the very edge of the contained property. With a sweep of her hand, Tillie said, "Many farmers have made the journey to join with us and tend to *his* fields. As is the natural priority, the men guide the nuns in caring for God's bounty, producing crops that feed the committed. It is important work."

"The committed?"

"Those who believe in the Reverend's divine right to lead God's people to heaven."

Dianna studied the woman's face. Was she a true believer or was she merely playing a role? Dianna was unable to tell. "And what of *The Chosen*? How do they serve Reverend John?"

"At his feet, indulging his pleasure, worshipping his essence, tending to his personal needs so that he is free to commune with the Lord and his people. It is a privilege to be called to serve him. Very few are. He loves openly, but he trusts few."

OMG. She is sleeping with him. Maybe she isn't undercover.

Dianna's gaze traveled around the fields. The scene wasn't much different from that of workers tending to the fields in America, just warmer and more humid. She tried to gather her thoughts. "So, what is the difference between the nuns and *The Chosen*?"

"Most of the nuns have taken a vow of silence to ensure their focus remains solely on God's delight. They have shed all of their earthly vanities, those material things that would distinguish them or make them appear more worthy than others." She smiled at Dianna. "Material wealth means nothing here. We have abandoned the trappings of the past. Our nuns have embraced a path of service. They are essential to our community. They tend to the gardens and the fields, they teach and enlighten our children, they run the laundry and ensure all of our people are fed and clothed. No one wants for anything here. Everything is provided. Everyone contributes."

"So not all of the people are silent? I mean, how can they teach without speaking?"

Tillie shook her head. "It is not required, simply encouraged. And yes, with the education of the children, not wholly possible. All we ask is that they embrace the silence in reverence when possible. It is our practice to focus inward and when possible, embrace the silence. Meditation and prayer breed gentle hearts."

Dianna studied Tillie. This was not the same defiant woman she had befriended in Morocco. She appeared to truly believe. She remembered Cade's advice, "Question everything." Sadly, she had nothing but questions. She was tempted to tip her hand, but Dianna knew that could backfire. She simply could not risk blowing her cover.

Tillie led her to the other side of the mansion and gestured to a group of women gathered under the shade of a tree. They appeared to be sewing. "The mothers and wives must, of course, have the ability to communicate with their husbands and children. Their focus is on nurturing. They serve the Lord and Reverend John in their obedience to their husbands and families. Providing for their emotional and physical needs. They are not required to wear the nun's habit, but some choose to do so for comfort." She peered at Dianna. "Are you not comfortable in your attire?"

Dianna frowned. "I'm not sure. I feel as if I am wearing no clothing at all. The habit is light and cool, and I have not seen a single mosquito, so that's a plus. But it makes me feel anonymous . . . and naked."

Tillie nodded. "Exactly. Not better nor more blessed than others. One and the same. As it should be. No need to prove yourself, no need to stand out from the crowd, more room for just being you. Bliss in nothingness." The look in her eyes was sincere. "We are an oasis in a cruel world. A place where no one judges or is judged."

So, Tillie is drinking the Kool-Aid. Dianna felt her heart skip a beat. Then why hadn't she outed her? She knew her real name. Surely, she wondered why Dianna had been introduced as Bennie.

A loud scream startled Dianna from her musings. Tillie began to run and Dianna followed. A crowd had gathered in the far corner of the compound, near what appeared to be a well.

A woman dressed in a simple white housedress turned to Tillie, her eyes filled with panic. "I'm sorry. I should have watched him more carefully. He got away from me."

Tillie gently pushed the woman aside and peered into the well. "Bring me some rope. He is on a ledge. Far away from the bottom. For now." When she turned to the women to indicate she should move, Dianna peered over Tillie's shoulder.

The hissing was the first clue. The stealthy movement of

dark, writhing things, leaping into the air as if trying to snatch the boy's body, was the second. The well was filled with snakes. Poisonous ones by their markings. *A Viper's pit.* A feeling of unease overcame Dianna. What's a viper's pit doing in an area filled with people, especially children?

Anders waited anxiously as the bus unloaded. Something was wrong. He could feel it. When Cate walked off the bus alone, he frowned. "Where's Bennie?"

Cate shrugged. "She wasn't in her room this morning. I was told she was sick and they had taken her to their Infirmary. She wasn't feeling well last night. I told her it was all that *DEET* she was dousing herself in. They let us soak in their communal bath. She seemed better after that. I mean once she got all that crap off her skin. But I haven't seen her since then." Cate's eyes narrowed and she leaned forward to whisper in Anders' ear. "Last night we discovered the place was run by God's Delight and they knew I was coming. I want to leave, but . . . I have a really bad feeling about this."

Alex called to her and Cate danced over to Alex, flinging herself at him as if she hadn't a care in the world. Anders frowned. Why isn't she expressing her concern to Alex?

Maybe she doesn't trust him after all.

Anders tried to quell his panic. *Why is Dianna the only one not returning to the orphanage? Is she really sick?* He walked over to Alex. "Hey, be right back. Nature calls." Anders entered the dormitory and headed to the restroom. He walked into a stall, shut the door, and reached behind the toilet seat, removing the burner phone he had taped there. He turned on the power and held up the phone. Thank God for satellites. Three bars. A cell phone would never have worked in the jungle. Thinking that they would remain together, Anders and Dianna had opted for only one phone. That was a mistake. They had failed to anticipate that they could be separated. How had he missed the age-old strategy — *divide and conquer?* Cults often used isolation or the threat thereof to bend people to their will. Why would God's Delight be any different?

Hurriedly, Anders typed, "2 *reported sick. GD HQ. Status unknown."* He pushed send.

Anders waited a minute. A soft chime sounded. The reply read, "2 *has issued no alerts. Assume mission not compromised. Patience."* Anders grasped the phone, angry. Dammit, this was his wife, possibly in danger. And all they could say was, *Patience?*

Anders struggled to calm himself. They were right — he was overreacting. Dianna was well-trained. She had a level head. She knew how to initiate an extraction. He had to trust her ability to protect herself and do her job. And the best way for him to protect her was to make sure her cover remained intact. Suddenly, he understood why Janet had removed herself from the field after falling in love with Cade. Not being able to protect your partner tore at your heart. He knew he needed to focus on the job, not Dianna. But damn, it sure wasn't easy.

Anders typed, *RT.* Roger that. He powered off the phone and re-taped it to the back of the toilet. Then he flushed and exited the stall. *Please God, keep her safe.*

Dianna watched as Tillie instructed the young boy to loop the rope around his waist and hang on. With the help of two burly guards, the boy was carefully pulled from the inside of the well.

His now dirty face was streaked with tears. The boy ran to his mother. "Momma, I wasn't bad." The boy looked around in panic and declared, "The devil pushed me. To feed the snakes." He sobbed again. "Like that man who said he wanted to leave—"

His mother hushed him and led him away. The boy continued to cry. "I wasn't bad, Momma. I promise. I love Reverend John." He looked over his shoulder at the crowd, and wailed. "I am not evil . . ."

Tillie flushed, her look guarded. "Guess the snakes scared the poor boy. He'll have nightmares for sure."

Dianna glanced at the well, then at Tillie. "Why are there snakes in the well with children around, anyway? Isn't that a bit dangerous?"

"There are a lot of snakes around here. Sometimes they wander onto the grounds looking for food. We have people trained to remove any animals that could pose a danger to our community. They usually throw them back into the jungle. However, vipers and coral snakes are poisonous and are not so easily deterred. Remove them and they are likely to come right back. So we throw them into the well. It's deep enough so they can't escape. And since we don't feed them, they eat each other. Survival of the fittest, I guess." She shrugged. "The children know to stay away. They are reminded constantly. Some just don't listen. Daniel is lucky he didn't have to pay the consequences."

"But he saw a man thrown down the well?"

Tillie laughed, but her eyes narrowed. "Daniel has a vivid imagination. Why would we throw anyone into a well filled with poisonous snakes?"

Why indeed? Dianna studied the well. The hiss of the snakes was unnerving. However, to a child, they would warrant investigation, a sort of attractive nuisance. Yet there was no fence around it to keep the curious away. Or any grate covering the opening. Was it possible they were using it to generate fear?

Dianna cast her gaze around the courtyard. This community was pretty peaceful, almost abnormally so. Her father was fond of saying *Some people are just going along to get along.* Meaning it was easier to comply than fight. Was that what was happening here? Or was it something more? Dianna inwardly sighed. She shouldn't judge people because their community was outside her normal experience. She had to make an assessment based on fact. She needed more information.

The crowd began to disperse. Tillie led Dianna over to the long one-story building. It was clearly a school. Children played on swings, a jungle gym, and a slide, while women supervised. She turned to Dianna. "This is a full-grade school. The teachers focus on the younger children, but the older students participate in long-distance learning. We have computers and access to the Internet. Our facilities are quite modern."

"What about college or learning a trade?"

Tillie shook her head. "There is no need. We are self-sustaining. Higher education serves no purpose here. Even our medical staff is self-trained."

"But everyone can leave when they want, right?"

Tillie cocked her eyebrow, clearly amused. "Of course. But why would they? This is paradise."

"It is indeed, darling Miranda," drawled a deep sultry voice. A tall, well-built man dressed in a white cossack, a thick wooden cross draped around his neck, wrapped his arms around her and kissed her cheek. His loose, long blonde hair framed a tan, handsome face with a strong nose and a wicked, full-lipped grin. He turned his piercing blue eyes toward Dianna and smiled. "Hello," he said.

The man studied her, his expression predatory.

Dianna shifted uncomfortably. *So, Tillie is using another name. Meaning she's undercover. Noted.* Dianna stuck out her hand and said. "Hi, I'm Bennie. I'm one of the students from

Wisconsin working over at the orphanage. You were kind enough to allow us to stay here."

The man took her hand and stroked it, his expression suddenly thoughtful. "Tell me, *Bennie from Wisconsin*, what do you think of my paradise?" His hand moved to her lower arm.

Dianna flushed. *My paradise? Is this Reverend John?* "It's beautiful. Peaceful. But hot. And humid. *Really* humid." She gazed up into the man's eyes, somewhat stunned at the lust she found there. *My God, he looks like he wants to devour me.* Dianna quickly looked away.

The man chuckled. "You get used to it. But we keep the air-conditioning on in the dormitories for the newbies and limit their time in the sun. And of course, we all take a siesta during the hottest part of the day if we need one." He released her arm. "We worship at day's end when the air begins to cool. Otherwise, things get a little . . . sweaty." He leaned down and kissed her on the cheek, gently tugging her hair. Then he walked away. Dianna's gaze did not leave him as children followed him, playfully competing for his attention. *Just like Jesus.*

He was flirtatious with the women but kind and indulgent with the children. His presence was compelling. And the fact that he could pass for one of the wild Alphas on the cover of a romance novel probably didn't hurt either. The man turned and smiled at her. Dianna said, "I take it that's Reverend John?"

Tillie nodded. A strange expression crossed her face. She whispered, "He is going to send for you now. I can tell. You need to be careful." She smiled at Reverend John and said loudly. "Come, it's time for lunch and then a siesta. You've been out in the heat all morning. I don't want you to get sick."

Dianna and Tillie sat down for a lunch of fruit salad, some sort of dark bread, and a brownie. As Dianna sipped from a bottle of water, her gaze swept the room. She had spotted about ten of the missing students, but she knew there had to be more. "How many people are actually here?" she asked.

Tillie paused and thought. "Well, there are about three hundred members total, but not all live here. Some work on missions around the area, such as the orphanage. Others work with our primary benefactors in the United States, setting up our tours of the college campuses and our fundraisers."

Dianna chewed on her brownie and yawned, the heat and a wave of fatigue overtaking her. "Wow, I guess you were right about the heat. I am about to fall asleep."

Tillie smiled. "Our cooks use a lot of native herbs and spices in our foods, some found in the jungle, some grown here. We believe they promote wellness and help prevent disease. However, one of them—*Caapi*—can make you sleepy. But a good sleepy. You'll have a pleasant nap."

As Dianna struggled with her desire to sleep, her mind began to wander. *Caapi.* She knew that plant. A red flag waved in her brain, but she couldn't hold on to it. What had she been told about it? She stood and yawned again. "I'd better get to my room before I pass out."

Dianna woke up slowly. She opened her eyes and frowned. Her room felt different. Her bed felt different. She felt different. She squinted at the ceiling. The room was bathed in that strange blue light again. How long had she slept?

Sluggish, she pulled herself into a seated position. The room was a bit fuzzy around the edges. Slowly, the noise that woke her seeped into her brain. Chanting. Again. Confused, Dianna got up and opened her door. She peered out. One of the nuns looked up. Softly, she said, "We are going to worship. Join us." Without thinking, Dianna pulled the hood of her habit up over her head and joined the line.

She was thankful they walked slowly. She felt weak.

The nuns chanted, "He is God's vessel. Our leader into the divine light. We shall serve and prostrate ourselves before him. Our adoration is to God's delight."

Dianna took a few more steps.

"He is God's vessel. Our leader into the divine light. We shall serve and prostrate ourselves before him. Our adoration is to God's delight."

She began to mumble the words, her tongue tripping over the unfamiliar chant. The more she tried to speak, the easier it became, until finally, she proclaimed, "He is God's vessel. Our leader into the divine light. We shall serve and prostrate ourselves before him. Our adoration is to God's delight."

The nun in front of her turned and smiled. Dianna followed the procession into the courtyard. Music with an emphatic drum beat floated from unseen speakers. It was sensual, hypnotic, enthralling. The crowd was boisterous, some swaying, others making nonsensical proclamations. Some clothed, some not. All appeared to be in a joyous mood. Dianna frowned. It was almost as if they were under the influence . . . of something.

Reverend John and The Chosen were in the center of the courtyard. The naked women danced sensually, rubbing up against him, running their hands over his body as he kissed and groped them. One dropped to her knees and began to adoringly kiss his feet. The other women drifted away and he pulled her to her feet and led her to a highbacked armchair. He sat and pulled her into his lap, kissing and stroking her hair, then her breasts. Suddenly the woman appeared to grow younger, her features softening, her youth and innocence plain. A woman-child. No longer a teen, but not yet a woman. A virgin laid at Reverend John's altar?

Dianna found herself swaying to the beat, her mind drifting, small waves of pleasure coursing through her body. She watched the Reverend, envious of the woman who had caught his attention. Wanting to be the precious prize he cuddled on his lap. Confused, she frowned. No this wasn't right. Why was she feeling this way?

She shouldn't be here. She had a . . . a . . . A man's face flashed into her mind. He was tall and muscular with shaggy brown hair. His bright green eyes smiled at her, his full lips poised to . . . Dianna shook her head. What was happening to her? She felt like she was losing control.

A bonfire was lit and Reverend John stepped in front of it, a thick brown snake wrapped around his neck. His sculpted bronze body was fully on display. The Reverend pulled the snake's head from his body. He danced with it, taunted it, dodged the viper's tongue. His movements became more erratic as he praised God and defiled the devil. The snake's head seemed to move closer and closer to his neck, prepared to strike.

Many in the crowd grew frenzied. Dancing and shouting, their movements frantic, their words praising the Living Christ. Taunting the devil.

Suddenly, the snake lunged. Laughing, Reverend John cast it away from his body and into the fire. Then he collapsed onto the ground, his body writhing.

The crowd fell silent. Waiting. Watching. After several moments, Reverend John jumped to his feet, smiling. "Praise be to God!" he proclaimed. Several of The Chosen rushed to him, kissing him and his body, their relief apparent. They robed him and then, led him away.

The people around Dianna dropped to their knees, weeping, praising God, praising his Son, praising the Living Christ. Slowly, Dianna's mind began to clear. She hadn't seen this kind of fanaticism since her grandmother had dragged her to some sort of tent revival. Her parents had been livid when she told them about the snakes and the Pentecostal preacher. That had seemed crazy, but this, this was madness.

Silently, she inserted herself back into the line that was forming and followed the nuns back to her dormitory. No one acknowledged her as she snuck back into her room. Maybe no one had realized she didn't belong.

CHAPTER ELEVEN: THE PITCH

Someone was banging on her door. Dianna moaned. She just wanted to sleep. More knocking. "Go away," Dianna complained. Her eyes again closed and she went back to sleep.

Dianna heard her door open and sensed someone walking in.

"Dianna, wake up. The siesta is over."

Dianna dragged one eyelid up over what felt like a crusty eye and moaned again. Tillie appeared before her. "What are you doing here?"

"Sorry, I got worried. You've been sleeping for several hours. The siesta ended an hour ago—oh, the bus is fixed. I didn't know if you wanted to go over to the orphanage and work for a few hours."

Dianna's eyes opened. Confusion flooded her mind. "What day is it?"

Tillie smiled. "Wednesday. Same as three hours ago."

Dianna shook her head. "No. I went to something last night. There was a lot of dancing. And a snake. A big ugly brown snake. And Reverend John was naked and . . ."

Tillie giggled. "Wow. That must have been some dream."

Dianna shook her head again. "No, it was real. So real." Dianna yawned. "I'm so tired. I just want to sleep." She turned over to her left and closed her eyes.

She felt a pat on her arm. "Okay then. I'll tell your friends that you're still a bit under the weather."

Dianna heard a door close and sleep again overcame her.

The next morning, Dianna slowly opened her eyes. She still felt off, but God, she was hungry. Dianna got out of bed and sniffed at her habit—her clothing officially stunk.

Dianna walked to the restroom and relieved herself, then she used a bottle of water to wash her face and brush her teeth. She looked in the mirror above the sink and groaned. Her hair looked like it been attacked by an oil slick. It was practically plastered to her head. She studied her water supply. Not enough to wash her hair. And the dry shampoo wouldn't work either.

Reluctantly, Dianna turned on the shower and moved the handle to the middle. The last thing she wanted was a hot shower. She tossed off her habit and removed her money belt, then walked under the water. She was careful to keep any water off out of her eyes and off her face, and quickly washed her hair. Then she soaped up and rinsed her body.

As she dried her hair, someone knocked on her door. Dianna quickly wrapped a towel around her body and opened the door a crack.

"Ready?" Cate asked.

Dianna shook her head. "Just got out of the shower. Want to meet at breakfast?"

Cate nodded. "Sure, no rush, though. I guess the bus is out of service. We'll be spending the day here. I'm going to head to the communal bath after breakfast." She smirked. "The water in the showers is a little too hard for me. I still feel dirty."

"Be right there. Just have to comb out my hair and get dressed."

Cate nodded and walked away.

Dianna closed the door and leaned against it. The bus was broken? *Again? Seriously?* Anders would freak if she failed to show up another day. However, it wasn't like she had a choice. At least she would have more time to look around, perhaps find Merry Wright.

As Dianna reached inside her closet for her duffle bag, she noticed that a clean nun's habit had been hung there. She frowned. Sure, it was comfortable and she had remained cool and bug-free, but wearing the habit a second day might send the wrong message—that she wanted to join God's Delight.

Then she paused. Or maybe it might get others to let down their guard. She had people to find. Her street clothes would alert them that she was an outsider. A habit would not. She grabbed the habit and slipped it on. Then she combed out her hair and dried it, using a small hand dryer. The air was so humid it would never dry naturally. Dianna glimpsed into the mirror and smiled. *Better.*

She left her room and headed toward the dining room. When she arrived, she went through the line. Smiling at Fred, she said, "Good morning." She pointed to a tray of French toast. "Can I have some of that and some scrambled eggs, please?" He nodded and filled her plate. "Thanks, Fred." Dianna grabbed a bottle of apple juice and turned away from him, searching the room for Cate. She frowned. Cate wasn't there.

"Looking for your friend?" Tillie walked over to her. "She and the other girls headed over the communal baths. She said to tell you she would catch up with you later."

"Geesh. She couldn't wait ten minutes?"

Tillie laughed. "I got the sense she really wanted that bath."

Dianna sighed. "Well, okay. After I eat, I'll go look for her."

Tillie grabbed a mug and poured herself a cup of coffee. She offered one to Dianna. "The water is boiled by the machine, it's perfectly safe."

Dianna nodded. "I'll try it, but hot coffee in this climate just seems wrong."

Tillie smiled. "It actually helps you deal with the heat," she said. "Clears the mind." She motioned toward a table at the back of the room. Several of The Chosen was seated there. "Care to join us?"

"Why not? I hate eating alone."

"Don't we all?" Tillie led her toward the table. When they sat, Tillie smiled at the women. "Ladies, this is Bennie. She's working on that new shed at the orphanage. The bus broke down again, so she'll be staying behind today. Introduce yourselves."

A redhead with bright green eyes smiled. "We met you the other day. You were with Cate, right? I'm Lynn."

Dianna nodded. "Nice to meet you, Lynn."

A petite brunette with a shy smile and large brown eyes extended her hand. "I'm Rachel." She gestured toward the blonde next to her. "This is Ginnie." The woman waved a piece of toast at her.

Tillie handed her a cup of coffee. "Taste. We grind our own blend of beans here. So many different kinds are produced in the mountains. It's amazing."

Dianna took a sip. "Wow. That's really strong. Strong, but good. I'm surprised you don't have people running in circles from the jolt of caffeine.

Rachel laughed. "Actually, the caffeine content is rather light. Darker roasts have less caffeine and some of the coffee growers actually grow beans with lower caffeine content. So, you get the flavor, but not the rush or the headache a coffee addiction can cause. Instead, you get a rather luscious, flavor-filled brew." She smiled. "So much better than American coffee. I miss it when I visit the states."

Dianna took another sip. "I have to admit, it is delicious. Is this something I can get at the airport before I get on my return flight?"

Rachel smiled. "Not this blend. But maybe something similar."

"When do you plan on leaving?" Ginnie asked.

"I'm only here for a week."

"Wow, that's too bad. We could really use some help at the school. I was hoping we could convince a few of you to stay a bit longer."

Dianna tried to keep a neutral expression on her face. Was this part of the pitch? Finally, she said, "Well, I need to get back to school. It's my last semester. Maybe after I graduate, I could give you a few months." She smiled. "Who knows?" She finished her breakfast. "But I'm here today. Happy to help any way I can."

Rachel gazed at Ginnie. Some sort of silent communication seemed to pass between them. Then she smiled at Dianna. "That would be great." She stood. "Let's go."

Dianna stood and picked up her tray.

Tillie smiled at her. "Leave it. Someone else will get it."

Ah, a hierarchy. The Chosen don't do scut work.

As they walked from the dining area, Dianna couldn't help but notice how others moved out of their way, their heads bowed. *In respect? Or fear?* Inwardly, Dianna frowned. *Definitely a hierarchy.*

They walked through the grounds toward the school. The four women strode proudly past other members who milled about. They greeted no one and no one greeted them, but with their long hair, they definitely stood out. Just as they approached the school, Dianna heard a soft buzz. The four women stopped, each checking slim watches on their wrists.

Lynn smiled at Dianna. "I'm afraid we're being called back to the mansion. Why don't you come with us? After we deal with whatever problem has arisen, we can walk back to the school together."

Dianna nodded but said nothing. She followed the women to the imposing home. She tried to ignore the queasiness in her stomach, but she was once again feeling off.

Dianna was surprised at the elegance of the mansion. It was furnished simply, but luxuriously. Clearly, no expense had been spared. It was a bit disconcerting that everyone else lived in dormitories, while only a few lived on a grand scale. She followed the women down a dimly-lit hallway to a pair of dark wooden doors. Lynn knocked, then entered. The other women followed. Dianna stayed back, not sure whether she was meant to wait or follow.

Finally, Tillie stuck her head out the door. "It's okay. Come on in. This will just take a minute."

Dianna passed through the doors and tried not to gape. The room was set up like an operations center. Computers lined three walls, while a large white screen sat on the fourth. She asked Tillie, "What's this?"

"This is how we sustain our community." Reverend John swung around in an office chair and grinned at Dianna. "Bet you thought we lived in the dark ages, huh?" The four women tittered. "Although cell phones are banned and actually not operational here, our sustainability relies on our ability to monitor our business interests, which are worldwide."

Dianna studied the man. *International business interests?* Perhaps he wasn't just a simple preacher after all. She gazed around the room. *I definitely need to get a look at those computers.*

Reverend John continued, "At the moment, we are having problems with our satellite link. Probably sunspots or something." He stood and straightened his robes. "While my sweet sisters attempt to rectify the problem, why don't I show you around? I think you'll be impressed." He leered at Dianna. There was no escaping the intent behind his offer.

Oh, crap. Dianna pushed out a smile. "I'd love that." He

extended a hand and she took it.

He led her through another door and then to a small, but steep staircase. "Let's start at the top. The view up there is so much better than on the ground." He dropped her hand and led Dianna up the stairs. As he walked, his robe swung open, exposing long, lean legs. Dianna gulped. And no underwear.

Shit. Fuck. Damn. Was that intentional? Her brain scrambled to assess the situation. *Spy Craft 101. When faced with a potentially sexual situation, let it play out as far as your conscience allows, then vomit. Do not say no. Do not display outright rejection. Simply vomit.*

When they reached the top of the stairs, Reverend John again extended his hand, then gently pulled Dianna into a brightly lit alcove. "My version of a tower room," he said softly. "A place to get away from the day to day and contemplate."

Dianna moved around the room, gazing out of the floor to ceiling windows.

Reverend John placed a hand on her arm and moved closer. "My kingdom, as it were." He pointed. "We have over a hundred acres here. Some we farm, some are leased to other farmers."

Dianna looked at him, slightly stepping away from his body. "And what do you farm?" She turned back to the window.

"Whatever we need to remain self-sustaining. Food for my followers, feed for the animals, even some cotton and hemp for fabric. We need very little from the outside world." He kissed the back of Dianna's neck and wound his arm around her waist.

Dianna forced herself to remain calm. "And what do the other farmers grow?"

"Whatever they want. Some of illegal. But as long as they pay their rent on time, we don't interfere." Dianna felt the

Reverend's heated breath on her skin as he leaned in and sniffed. "If the authorities don't make an effort to police the drug trade, why should I?" He turned Dianna around. Then he ran a finger along her cheek. "So beautiful," he murmured. He kissed her.

Dianna trembled. *How long can I let this play out?*

Unfortunately, Reverend John mistook her discomfort for arousal. He tried to deepen the kiss, his hand now cupping her breast through the habit. He wedged a leg between her thighs.

Dianna shuddered. The queasiness in her stomach seemed to explode into a riot of pain. She moaned. "I think I'm going to be sick." Then Dianna slid down Reverend John's body to the floor and vomited on his bare feet.

Reverend John jumped away from her and scowled. "Shit!" His glared at her. "What the hell, woman?"

Dianna grabbed her stomach. *Oh my, God. The pain!* She vomited again, then again. *Oh, crap. I really am sick.* Dianna curled up into a ball and groaned. "So sick," she muttered. Her last thought was, *Anders, help me.* Then she passed out.

Chapter Twelve: The Bat Signal

"What do you mean the buses are broken?" Anders demanded. "They have two. Both can't be out of service."

Mike shrugged. "Well, the bus that has been running between here and the nun's compound is out of service. I have no idea where the other bus is. From the sounds of things, those nuns travel all over the place."

"It doesn't bother you that we haven't seen Bennie for two days and now the other women are missing as well?"

"They're not missing, man. We know where they are." Mike laughed and clapped him on the back. "Hey, we're in the middle of the jungle. Things don't always work here. Engines rust out, the humidity fucks up gas lines. And did you see those tires? They looked like balloon tires, though I can't imagine where you could buy any here. It's only a day. Relax. We are ahead of schedule on the shed. We don't need the women anyway. I am sure they are enjoying their day off."

Anders studied the man. He had so little concern for the welfare of Dianna and the others, it was disconcerting. It was also suspicious. He stalked over to Alex. "Hey, the bus isn't coming today. I'm worried about the women."

Alex nodded. "Yeah, something's wrong with the bus. I guess it can't be helped. I just hope it's ready for our departure. I want to head home." He swiped at some sweat on his forehead. "At least now we'll be able to manage with the water we have left, but we're still going to cut it close."

Anders frowned. *Is this guy for real?* "Aren't you worried about Cate, Bennie, and the others?"

Alex laughed. "About as much as they are worried about us. They're living like queens." He smiled at Anders. "The bus will be fixed and then we'll meet them at the airport. No worries."

Anders asked, "Can we at least call them, make sure *everything* is really okay?"

Alex patted him on the back. "God, when did you become such an old grandma? Besides, the nuns have no phones. They're a silent order, remember? We can't do much until the bus gets fixed. Because if there's no bus, there's also no nuns to explain what's going on. My advice? Let's not worry until we have a reason to. Those buses are antiques. I'm not surprised they are so unpredictable."

"Wait a minute. If the nuns have no phones, how did we learn the bus was out of service and they weren't coming?"

Alex studied him, then frowned. "I have no idea. I'm sure no one walked through the jungle. All I heard was that they had sent a message. Maybe someone on a scooter?"

Anders wanted to slap Alex upside the head. *Way to be the leader.* Either the guy was being intentionally dense, or he was truly a doofus. "I'm going to hit the john before we get started working." He walked back to the dormitory. When he got inside the stall in the restroom, he sat on the toilet and removed the burner phone taped behind the tank. His hand shook as he powered the device. First, Dianna was sick. Today, the bus was out of operation. Something was up. He just knew it.

He typed *no bus 2day, 5 missing. Any info?* He pressed send and waited. The phone chimed and he read the message. *Checking. DNGI.* Do not get involved? Anders dropped his head into his hands. *Fuck.*

Dianna's eyes flew open. She squinted, trying to make out shapes in the blue light. Somehow, her bed had been moved and the dresser was now on the opposite side of the room. Slowly, she pulled the mosquito net aside and sat up. She stared at an empty wrist. Where was her watch? Oh, no. She needed it to . . . Dianna stumbled to her feet and stood. This wasn't her room. Sometime during the day or night, she had been moved.

In place of the closet, a heavy armoire stood. Dianna walked to it and opened the doors. Several of the nun's habits hung inside. Dianna squatted and felt around the floor. Her duffle bag was gone. While facing the cubicle, she felt around her waist. They'd also taken her travel wallet. Her papers. Her pills. Her gun. What the hell? A shadow in the back of the armoire moved. Hands reached for her. The shadows shifted. They shook and the chains that manacled their hands rattled. Dianna quickly closed the doors.

Another door opened and a nun entered, carrying a tray. She smiled at Dianna and began to dance, delicately balancing the tray, bringing the food just close enough so that she got a whiff, a scent. Oh, food, glorious food. The nun offered her a banana and Dianna hurriedly wolfed it down. She reached for another, but the nun shook her head. She offered Dianna some sort of brown liquid in a cup. Something tugged at Dianna's memory. "Don't drink it. It will make you sick. Or maybe it will make you sleep." Yes, she wanted to sleep . . . Dianna gulped it down.

"Dianna," a voice whispered. "You're in trouble. Call for help. The bat signal, Dianna. Use the bat signal." She shook her head, trying to clear it, and mumbled. "What? I don't understand."

The voice said, "Run, Dianna. Hide. Protect yourself. Come on, you know how. The bat signal."

Dianna's stomach growled again. God, she was so hungry. She needed steak and a big old Idaho potato and a beer. Oh yes, a beer. Dianna licked her lips. She was so thirsty. She looked at the nun holding the cup and reached for it again. But the nun merely smiled and disappeared.

Dianna winced. God, her throat hurt. Dianna tried to swallow.

She was so thirsty, so dry. The voice urged, "You're in trouble, Dianna. Use the bat signal . . ."

Suddenly, her room lit up. Oh, so many colors! It blinked and it pulsed. Like a dance club. Then the noise started. Odd screeches, short blasts of music. Heavy metal. Throbbing. She covered her ears. My God, that hurts. "Please stop." She fell onto the floor, her body curled into a protective ball and clapped her hands over her ears. "Stop," she sobbed. "Please stop."

Silence. The room went dark. Then a voice. She knew that voice. "I will protect you, Bennie. I will bring you delight. I will show you the way to the eternal path. Let me save you, Bennie. Place yourself in my hands. Reach out. Take my hand. Call to me. I will save you. I am your savior. Only I can save you . . ."

Dianna moaned and struggled to think. "Who's Bennie?" she muttered. Dianna reached out. Someone grabbed her hand, then pushed her. Suddenly, she was falling. Desperately Dianna tried to stop the descent, clawing at the walls as they raced past her. Then she heard it. The rattle of snakes.

Dianna screamed.

Dianna sat up. Her eyes were out of focus and she had a blazing headache.

A hand gently pushed her back into a laying position. "Shhhhh," Tillie said. "You've been very sick. You had a terrible fever. Just rest."

Dianna blinked and tried to open her eyes. It hurt so much. Then she remembered the voice. *The bat signal, Dianna. The bat signal.*

With her tongue, Dianna reached into the back side of her mouth. There it was, the bat signal. She bit down but didn't have the strength to keep the pressure on for the required length of time. Instead, she drifted back into delirium.

The loud beep forced Cade's attention from the report MISix

had forwarded to him. *Dianna.* He hit a few keys on a laptop and a map of the God's Delight compound appeared. He frowned. "Where is she?" He typed another key. "Come on. Where are you, Dianna?" He ran a hand through his hair, frustrated. "They have to be jamming the signals." He turned from his seat in the surveillance van, his gaze settling on Harry.

The man shook his head as he frowned at his computer screen. "How did the signal even get through? There was a quick blip in one the buildings, then nothing." Harry gazed at Cade. "You sure that was her bat signal? She's supposed to clamp down on it for two minutes. That was barely thirty seconds. It might just be an anomaly."

Cade gritted his teeth and pushed a few buttons on his laptop. "Anders hasn't seen her for four days. Something's wrong. I can feel it. There is no way she'd go silent for that long. Dammit, I knew I should have ordered a pussy pack." A pussy pack was an Agency-specific monitoring package that involved the placing of tracking chips in each orifice.

"The threat assessment was so low, it wasn't even considered," Harry said. "This was supposed to be a simple in and out. Besides, Anders was supposed to be with her."

Cade scowled. "Her last name is Murphy, as in Murphy's Law? Anything that can go wrong, will. Dammit, we should have done a better job of anticipating. We didn't know what we were going into. We had no information."

Harry ran a hand through his hair. "Boss, you sent in two highly qualified agents to collect basic information. That was it. Unless Dianna got involved in something she wasn't prepared for, there is no way this should have gone bad. Hell, she has her tool kit. Her last best option is to leave the compound and signal for backup . . ." Harry frowned. "Unless she's somehow incapacitated. Dammit. What about backup agents?"

Cade groaned. "We were relying on Anders and MISix. MISix won't be much help. They're more concerned with finding an errant royal who got religion. And all Anders has been told is that she was sick. How sick, we don't know. She may no longer be sick, just in danger."

"Well, she hasn't shown up at the orphanage for four days. They're scheduled to leave Bolivia in two days. Why not just wait it out? If she doesn't show up on Saturday, then go in."

"You're missing the point, Harry," Cade snapped. "An agent may have requested extraction. That means we go in now."

Harry glared at him. "And how do you suggest we do that, boss? It took the Agency almost a week to figure out how to pull me out from that Bolivian prison. At least you knew where I was."

"We're going to have to go in blind. We're not dealing with skilled guerillas here. They're religious zealots. Only the guards have weapons. Agent Murphy has asked for help, and she's going to get it. The Agency guarantees that for each and every mission. We're not going to stop now."

Anders raked the gravel around the completed storage shed. *Dammit, I need to get to Dianna.* The sounds of tires on the packed dirt caused him to turn and watch as an official-looking Jeep pulled into the courtyard. Three men. Two armed. *Could this day get any worse? If we get in trouble with the police, I'll never get to Dianna.*

The two men bearing guns jumped out of the vehicle and began yelling, "*Americanos!* Show yourselves."

Mike muttered, "Oh, shit. What now?"

Anders studied him. "Has this happened before?"

Mike shook his head. "The locals have never given us any trouble. Just stay calm. They'll probably just check our visas and leave."

The two men approached the group. In heavily accented English, one of them demanded, "Identity papers, please." The other man just scowled. His hands held steady as he pointed his handgun at the group.

Anders and the others pulled their visas from pockets and wallets, and one by one showed them to the officer.

When he got to Anders, the man studied the paperwork, then examined Anders' face. He frowned. "Do you have a passport?"

Anders shook his head. "No, they collected them on the plane."

The policeman conferred with his companion in whispered, rapid-fire Spanish. Then he looked at Anders, his expression smug. "You will come with us."

Mike's eyes widened in alarm. "Wait, no. I can vouch for him. He's an American like the rest of us." He grabbed the policeman's arm. "For God's sake, tell us what you need and we'll get this straightened out."

The policeman sneered. "Remove your hand, now. We are bringing this man in for questioning."

Mike paled and stepped back.

The policeman grabbed Anders' arm roughly and said, "You will come with us." He glared at Mike. "And we may be back for more." His mouth curled up into a cruel grin. "Passports or jail? You choose."

Anders knew better than to tangle with the local police. He allowed the man with the gun to push him toward the Jeep. Hopefully, all it would take was one quick call to the U.S. Embassy and he would be released. Still, it was strange that he had been singled out. It was almost as if the police were looking for him. *Has my cover been blown?*

The officer led Anders back to the Jeep and forced him into the backseat. The other policeman slid in next to him, his gun aimed at Anders' belly. A third man started the Jeep and turned out of the compound. Anders gazed at the back of the head of the driver. Then his gaze moved to the man's fingers. The nails were clean and trimmed, and there was a wedding ring with a singular stone, black onyx. As they sped down the road, Anders began to laugh.

"Oh my God, Cade," he choked out. "You had me going for a minute. What the hell, man? You couldn't approach me like a normal guy?" He sobered. "Oh, crap. If you pulled me out of there, Dianna's in trouble. Dammit, I knew she was in trouble. We have to get her out." He knew he was panicking, but this was his wife. He should never have allowed her to be shipped off to that compound alone.

The man next to him put away his gun and relaxed. The man in the front seat turned and studied him. Finally, Cade said, "Dianna sent up the bat signal, we think. Something may be wrong, or maybe not. But I'm not willing to take that chance. We're going in tonight."

Anders tried to remain calm. He nodded. "Good, because I was probably going to do something really stupid — like steal a scooter and head over there myself."

Cade glanced up at Anders in the rearview mirror. "Which is why Janet and I no longer work together. Hard to keep your head in the game when your wife's in trouble, isn't it?"

He downshifted and the Jeep lurched forward. "Our orders are to extract, then execute a mandatory welfare check for all Americans in the compound. We've gone as far as we can with this. The President is tired of pussyfooting around.

"I figured you'd want to lead the team that's doing the extracting."

CHAPTER THIRTEEN: EXTRACTION

Cade, Anders, and a team of seven men in military fatigues gathered around a small table in a run-down Bolivian hotel room.

One of the men smirked. "Nice set-up, boss. I think the brothel down the street might actually be an upgrade."

Cade scowled. "I grabbed what I could find. I apologize if your gentlemanly sensibilities are offended. While you might have preferred the brothel, I was not in the mood to pay off all the workers for their silence."

He gestured at a map of the God's Delight compound. "Let's get down to business. We don't have a lot of time. According to MISix, the God's Delight compound has a minimum-security force. Twenty armed guards divided among three shifts. At night, only four guards make the rounds. We've been led to believe that although the compound houses about three hundred people, the cult members are pretty complacent and once it's lights out, they stay out until morning."

"Why not just show up at the main gate and force our way in?" Anders swiped the sweat off his brow. "A flash grenade. A ram to the gates. We're in."

Cade sighed. "And alert the rest of the compound and the off-duty guards that they're under attack? You'd be slaughtered. People may be sleeping, but that doesn't mean they don't have access to weapons." His expression was one of reproach. "You aren't thinking rationally. I don't need you going off half-cocked and pulling a Rambo." Cade shook his head. "You have to remember that Dianna is only one piece of the puzzle. We still need to secure the compound for a welfare check. We need to be smart about this. We can't risk another Jonestown or a Waco." He pointed at Anders. "You will not be the match that sets off the powder keg."

Anders flushed and nodded. "Then how do we find Dianna? And how do we get her out of there without anyone noticing?"

"I'll get to that. But if Dianna is sick, as claimed, you need to start with the Infirmary. However, if she's not there, you will need to find her room and, unfortunately, we have no idea where that is. We do know that she is in this dormitory." He pointed to a building.

"Why not start with her room, then?" one of the men asked.

Cade pointed at the map. "Because as far as we can tell, the signal we received, however brief, came from the Infirmary."

Anders felt his eyes begin to tear. *Dammit. A Navy Seal doesn't show emotion.* He cleared his throat. "What if we're too late?"

Cade sighed and he tried to hide his worry. "Pray we're not."

Cate peered around a corner and patiently watched the hallway. She was pretty sure Bennie was in one of these rooms, but which one? She had heard some of The Chosen whispering about her. Things sure had gone to hell in a handbasket. Bennie was no longer in her room and she hadn't made it onto the bus to the orphanage the second day. Now, for the last two days, they'd claimed the bus wasn't operational. Something was up.

She'd seen both of the buses leave the compound since

then. The old mechanical problems excuse was obviously a lie. Cate was quite sure they were being kept at the compound for a reason. And knowing what a snake Reverend John was, it probably wasn't a good one. Was the man capable of kidnapping? Certainly, especially since it wasn't possible to walk out the front gate. They were in the middle of a jungle, for heaven's sake. Far away from civilization. It was going to be a matter of survival of the fittest. And one thing Cate knew how to do was survive.

Still, she couldn't figure out how she and Bennie had fallen into this trap. Reverend John had boldly expressed his interest when they met in Madison and had attempted to pursue her. She had cut him off and shut him down. That should have been the end of it. No one had even mentioned the cult when she signed up for the trip to the orphanage. As far as she knew, no one at Tau Omega Psi even knew of her connection. Still, if the compound had been used to house women on other trips, the link to God's Delight was not hidden. Someone was aware of it and she was willing to bet that someone was Mike. Had he worked with the dear Reverend to ensure Cate made the trip?

Still, even if she had been set up, that didn't account for Bennie and the other three girls. Bennie was on her own. She had no money. And the other girls—Lisa, Amy, and Sarah—seemed to be of modest means as well. So kidnapping them for ransom made no sense. Unless Reverend John had plans to make money off of them in another way. Cate cringed. Yeah, Reverend John was capable of selling or trading them for financial gain. Or maybe he just wanted more women for himself. Still, none of the girls were pushovers. She couldn't see any of them volunteering to stay, even for Reverend John. What was the benefit? No one really wanted to be stuck in a Third World country as a slave—which the cult members surely were—no matter the size of Reverend

John's penis.

It just didn't make sense. And that sent all sorts of bells going off. Somehow, Cate had to make sure all of them were on that plane back to the States, even if she had to get Bennie there in an ambulance. While The Chosen had proudly shown her their computer room, they hadn't been smart enough to hide their satellite phone. If she couldn't connect to the Internet via her phone, using their Wi-Fi, she could power up the satellite phone and send an alert to the powers that be. It was a secret number, completely untraceable, but once the call was transmitted, it would pinpoint her location. They would be on that plane back home, but first, she had to find Bennie.

Cate slowly moved into the hallway and, one by one tried the handle of each door. The third wasn't locked. She put her ear against it and heard movement inside. Gently, she turned the knob and pushed the door open, just a sliver. A nun was bent over a bed where someone was sleeping. When the nun moved aside, Cate withheld a gasp. Bennie lay there unmoving, deathly pale.

She couldn't tell what the nun was doing, but the room was bathed in a blue light. Cate frowned. Bennie had complained about that light. Could that be what was making her sick? Cate thought back to all the defense classes she had been forced to attend as a child. What were the rules for breaking victims? Desensitization. Block anything that could stimulate or comfort the senses. Light. Noise. Food. Heat. Sleep. Companionship. Cate frowned. If that was intent of the blue light and keeping Bennie isolated in this room, then maybe Bennie wasn't sick at all. Maybe they were brainwashing her.

Carefully, Cate closed the door. She crept down the hallway and headed back to her room. When she rounded a corner, she slammed into a body. She looked up and held back a scream. *Oh, shit!*

"Well, hello, lover. I've been looking for you." Dressed in only a white bathrobe, Reverend John smiled at her. "What have you been up to?"

Cate flung her arms around his neck and buried her head into his chest. She burst into tears. "I've been looking everywhere for you," she sobbed. "My roommate, my best friend, Bennie, is missing. I haven't seen her for days. They told me she was sick, but now I'm worried she's dead or something." Cate wailed, "I'm so worried. Where can she be?" She pulled at his robe and snuck a hand inside, gently stroking his chest. "Please, please help me. I have to find her."

Reverend John's wrapped his arms around her and his hands began to roam. He kissed her. "Of course," he said softly. His eyes were already glazed with lust. "I will see what I can do." He led her to her room.

Cate steeled herself. *I can do this. For Bennie.*

Cade turned to his combined team of U.S. Navy Seals and Agency personnel. "Okay. Before going in, you need the backstory. We believe more than one hundred American college students are located within the God's Delight compound. There also may be other men, women, and children who are U.S. citizens. We have confirmed about two hundred fifty people reside there. We don't know if the Americans are there willingly or not. Their families claim the latter, but since we just found the compound, we haven't had the opportunity to conduct a welfare check or even determine if one is needed. That's what Agent Murphy's job was. Obviously, that mission has failed.

"However, we can't take a chance that the place will implode if the people inside are threatened. We need to extract Agent Murphy quickly and cleanly. I do not want her or any other Americans to become collateral damage.

"You need to be aware there may be some psychological factors in play at the compound — techniques and tactics that could make Reverend John's followers revolt if threatened by outside forces. It is important to remember that while members of the cult may not be restrained *physically*, they may be restrained *psychologically*. For example, it is not uncommon for a cult to claim members can leave freely at any time. They just make it almost impossible to do so. Intimidation, peer pressure, threats of violence against family members back in the U.S., even a promise of imprisonment, or worse, death, may be used to control or break free will.

"In addition, cults tend to isolate themselves physically and socially. That not only prevents outside observation and intervention, it also blocks interaction with people who may suspect something is amiss and trigger dissension or an investigation." Cade pointed at the map of the compound. "God's Delight is physically isolated for a reason. Even if people want to leave, they are in the middle of the jungle. They have nowhere to go. Without physical transportation, it is unlikely that they could safely reach a populated area, and even if they did, God's Delight appears to have a broad reach. They do a lot of good works in the area. My bet is that the beneficiaries are unlikely to assist someone who is fleeing the cult."

Cade studied the extraction team. "We have also learned that God's Delight confiscates the passports of its members, purportedly holding them for security reasons. So even if someone does get out and reaches civilization, without identity papers, they could wind up in prison. In addition, it's about fifteen hundred miles to the closest U.S. Embassy. Walking there is impossible, and without money or papers, any other kind of travel is impossible. So, while leaving may be possible, once a cult member walks out those gates, they face almost insurmountable odds."

"Wouldn't that make our intervention more welcome?" Anders asked. "We offer the prospect of freedom."

Cade shook his head. "Under normal circumstances, maybe. Unfortunately, according to reports from the MISix agent embedded there, evidence points to some form of mind control, and we don't know how deeply entrenched it is. For example, most of the members are addicted to a plant called *Banisteriopsis Caapi* or *Caapi*. The locals believe it protects them from a variety of illnesses and boosts their immune system. They also believe it purifies their water, so it is used to filter water in indoor plumbing. It is also used in teas and as an herb in a variety of foods. If used regularly, it is believed to have a calming effect, similar to an antidepressant or anti-anxiety medication. And if smoked, it can have a hallucinogenic effect, similar to peyote or LSD." Cade smirked. "Think about it—there is no better way to control the masses than to keep them stoned. Especially when those people have no idea they are under the influence."

Anders groaned. "Dianna said everyone seemed happy and docile. Guess that's why."

Cade nodded. "And studies show when threatened, people under the influence either submit or get violent." He gazed at the group. "Obviously, the drug makes people suggestible. It has broken down people's resistance to authority. That enables a few people to lead while a whole lot follow. All it would take is a word from Reverend John and we could have a violent, full-scale revolt on our hands."

Another soldier said, "Which is why we're not to stir the kettle, just get Murphy out."

Cade nodded. "Your primary mission is to assess the welfare of Agent Murphy and if necessary, remove her from the scene. Once that's done, if feasible, you will secure the compound for a welfare check. That check will be conducted by an independent humanitarian agency, under the protection of an international security force." Cade pointed to the map again. "Now it seems the best way to access the compound is through this well . . ."

Chapter Fourteen: Extracting Dianna

A nders nodded at his team. Then he dropped down and crawled into the concrete pipe leading from the hot spring to the God's Delight compound.

The water surrounded him immediately. He allowed himself to drift, waiting for his mask to fog. It remained clear. Good. He gestured to his team to follow. The pipe was about three feet wide and seemed slightly declined. Anders floated away from the spring easily, occasionally using an arm or a leg to keep from bumping into the side. He arrived at a turn and Anders held up his hand, trying to recall the map in his mind. Just around the corner, the well should appear overhead.

He slid around the corner and looked up. *Holy crap. Was that . . .* Anders rose up on his knees to get a better look, his head now out of the water. The grate that supposedly filtered the water into the well was clogged with snakes, their angry rattles amplified by the water. *God, I hate snakes.* They were a fact of life as a Navy Seal, but snakes were irrational creatures. When threatened, they reacted instinctively. Some fled. Others attacked. Not only did the poisonous ones bite, but some were also quite skilled at choking the life out of you. While their diving suits were supposed to protect from snake bites, they would not protect his team from garroting by the reptile.

Anders treaded water. There had to be a better option. No

way was he opening the grate and releasing those snakes into the water. There were calculated risks and then there were stupid risks. Even Cade would agree that subjecting his team to the wrath of angry snakes was beyond stupid. Anders visualized the map. There was another pipe that led to some sort of pool. Was it wide enough? He had no choice but to find out. He needed to get to Dianna. Anders turned to the team, pointed upward, and wiggled his hand, indicating snakes. He shook his head and pointed to the left. Then he ducked back under the water and guided his men toward the pool.

The pipe began to narrow until they reached another grate, this one made entirely of mesh. Rather than cut through it, Anders pulled a tool off his belt and removed it, then passed it to the man behind him. It would continue on to the last man, who would refasten it. Anders shuddered. How many snakes had made their way into the pool?

Anders continued to swim through the narrowed passage. He made another turn, then came to an incline. Another grate appeared on the ceiling, this one with a small box at its side. Obviously, it was some sort of pump. Anders again used a tool to remove the grate and permitted it to float to the bottom of the pipe. Then he swam up through the opening into the pool. Although the lights were dim, he spotted legs and other body parts along one side. *Shit.* It should have been empty this late at night. He halted and as the other men moved into the pool, he motioned toward the legs floating in the water. Anders held up his fingers. *One. Two. Three.* As one, the team rose up and quickly unholstered their weapons from their waterproof containers, pointing them at the people gathered there.

Anders tried not to snicker. He removed his mask and peered at the three people before him. Reverend John was in the throes of passion as one woman rode his cock while another was engaged in some sort of underwater play. None of them noticed the presence of his eight-person team. Finally, he cleared his throat.

The woman riding Reverend John turned and upon spotting eight figures in black, quickly scrambled off of the Reverend's lap.

Reverend John's eyes flew opened and he lifted his head. "What the fuck, Candy," he growled. "Get back on my cock. You've barely started to get me off, cunt." Then he spotted Anders and his team. "Well, damn," he drawled. "Will you look at what the cat drug in?" He laughed. "Sorry, fellas. Not even these two can service all of you." He slapped the ass of the woman who was behind him, her head partially under water. "Although, Cookie here is pretty damn good at sharing all three holes."

A woman with long blonde hair and big blue eyes peered around his body.

Anders tried to hide his dismay. *Cate.*

Cate's eyes locked with his and she stood, the water falling directly onto Reverend John's face. Reverend John sputtered and yanked Cate into his lap.

Her expression coy, Cate snuggled into him. Then she laced her fingers into his neck and squeezed. In a matter of seconds, Reverend John slumped, his eyes drifting closed.

Anders pulled at his breathing tube. "What the hell was that, Cate?"

Cate smiled and stood. She turned to Candy and did the same. The woman slumped against the preacher. Cate climbed out of the pool, grabbed a robe piled next to it, and put it on. Pointing at Reverend John, she said, "Someone restrain that bastard, will you? Candy will need a gag. She's a mouthy one." Cate smirked. "But damn, the girl loves handcuffs and all sorts of kinky things. You might have some fun with her." Cate tossed her wet blonde hair over a shoulder and grinned at Anders. "Obviously, Mark, I too, have some *unusual skills.*"

She gestured toward his wet suit. "Kind of liking the ninja suit. Puts it all out there, for sure." Cate giggled. She gestured toward Anders. "Come on, I'll take you to Bennie. You just sped up my plan to get us out of here." Cate stopped and turned to Anders. "Do you have a spare weapon?" She smiled. "I couldn't really pack heat in this get-up."

Anders stared at her. "Do you even know how to use one?"

Cate grinned. "Certified on almost everything but assault weapons, though I am sure I could figure them out." She pointed at herself. "The State Department doesn't mess around with the families of diplomats. We know our weapons."

Anders pulled a pouch off of his leg and tossed it to her. "Defense only. You've only got five bullets. Use them wisely."

Cate nodded. She opened the pouch, pulled out a small pistol, and shoved it into the pocket of her robe.

Anders turned to his team. "Secure the prisoners, then lock this place down." His gestured to two men. "Palmer and Williams, you're with me. One of you stays with the prisoners. The rest of you move out and execute as assigned." He followed Cate out of the room.

They walked down a long corridor and through a locked door, a lock to which Cate had apparently filched the key. "They've got Bennie in the Infirmary. She's pretty sick and as far as I can tell, hallucinating. Not sure if she drank the water or they drugged her, but she needs help." Cate gazed at Anders and smiled. "Why am I not surprised that you're some sort of Ninja? Let me guess—FBI? CIA? Army? Navy? Marines?"

Anders snorted then said, "And what was that Ninja

move you just executed, Cate?"

Cate laughed. "Oh, I see, you're one of *those*." She shrugged. "I've been through every defense class you can imagine. I know how to take down kidnappers, terrorists, and assorted bad guys."

Anders nodded, but said nothing. "So where's the night security shift posted?"

Cate waved her hand. "Two of them patrol the mansion, the others stand at the gate. Though by now, they're all probably drunk off their asses and passed out. They all drink this shit brown brew that tastes like grain alcohol and packs one hell of a punch." She shuddered. "Scary stuff, but this place is so boring, they have nothing better to do."

"So, what's the deal with Reverend John?"

Cate grinned. "Just a little payback." She sighed dramatically. "But you interrupted before I could let my plan play out. Maybe later." She stopped in front of a closed door and pressed her fingers to her lips. Cate whispered. "She's in here."

Anders tried the door. It was locked. He pulled out a pick from his belt and knelt to open it.

Cate brushed him aside. She pulled a second key from the pocket of her robe. "So much easier with the key. Swiped this off of Reverend John." She inserted it into the lock, turned the doorknob, and pushed the door open.

A nun sleeping in a chair roused. Her eyelids fluttered, then her eyes flew open. She jumped to her feet, alarm clouding her face. One of Anders' men grabbed her and quickly wrapped a zip-tie around her wrists. Then he pushed her into the chair and let her feel the tip of his weapon. "One move, one scream, and it's all over, *chicka*," he whispered. The woman flinched but remained silent.

Anders' eyes swept the room. "What the hell's with the blue light?"

Cate shook her head. "Haven't been able to figure that one out yet, but Bennie claimed there was one in her room. I suspect if we looked around, we'd find more. The Soviets used blue light as a desensitization tool. Mind control." Cate scowled. "Dude has all sorts of books on brainwashing and mind control in his library. He's fascinated by that stuff. And since he needs cheap labor to run his kingdom, he's got to find some way to keep his troops in line." She cocked an eyebrow. "Bennie also mentioned something about white noise. There might be some sort of subliminal messaging going on. Chants, rants, rhymes, prayers. Send them through the walls when people are sleeping and the messages worm their way into their subconscious."

Anders shook his head. "Damn, Cate, you sound like you're . . ." *An agent, maybe of a lettered agency?* His comment died as Anders' gaze landed on the limp form on the twin bed. Fear consumed him. He rushed to Dianna. His hand wiped sweat-drenched hair from her face. He bent down and kissed her. *God, she's burning up.* "Babe," he crooned. "Babe, wake up."

Dianna's eyelids fluttered and clouded blue eyes gazed at him. She whimpered, then leaned over and vomited. Anders just managed to jump out of the way.

She frowned. Then she said in a raspy voice, "Daddy?"

Dianna frowned at the man leaning over her. Why was Daddy here? God, she hadn't seen him in ages. Not since . . . Dianna struggled to remember. Was it the Miss Wisconsin Pageant? That hadn't ended well. She had come in second. At least she had won some scholarship money, enough to pay her first year at law school. Dianna frowned. *Why was he here now? More importantly, where was she?*

Her eyes darted around the strange room. At that damn blue light. God, it made her head hurt. At a nun being restrained by a man in a black suit. *Really? That is so weird.* Dianna turned back to her daddy. Wait a minute. Daddy has blue eyes, not green. And his hair is gray, not light brown. The man smiled at her. Something tugged at her memory, but she couldn't quite catch it.

Dianna giggled. God, she had Wyatt Earped on some stranger's foot. *How embarrassing.* Suddenly, her focus shifted. The swirling lights were back. The ones that turned her stomach inside out. Dianna turned back to the stranger. He was bathed in an eerie light. *OMG. Is he an angel?* She blinked, trying to sharpen her focus. *No.* He was too magnificent to be a mere angel. Besides, he had no wings. He was dressed in black.

Panic overcame her. Was he death? Had he come to take her from Earth? Her eyes filled with tears. She wasn't ready. She wanted a man to love, children to nurture, a life. She mumbled, "No. You can't take me. I'm not ready . . . to die." Grief overcame her. Black was forcing out the light. *Mommy! Daddy! Don't let them take me.* Dianna groaned, then fell head first into nothingness.

Anders stared at Dianna, shocked. *What had just happened?* His wife didn't recognize him. In fact, she appeared to be terrified by the very sight of him. He glared at the nun. "What the fuck did you do to her?" The nun didn't respond. She just stared at the floor. Frustrated, Anders repeated the question in Spanish, *"Qué le hiciste a ella?"*

The nun lifted her head. Her eyes were filled with fear. Softly, she said, "I gave her water to drink. She has been so sick. Such a high fever. I didn't know what else to do."

Cate snorted. "You dumb shit. Your water's contaminated. You're used to it, she isn't. And you know that. By continually making her drink, all you did was make her sicker.

She probably had sunstroke. She would have recovered by the next day if you'd left her alone. Why didn't you bring someone from our group to take care of her? Are you trying to kill her?"

The nun sighed and took a deep breath. "I filtered the water. It should have been fine." She glared at Cate. "I'm not stupid. I did what I thought best. I was a CNA in America. We don't have traditional medical supplies here. We have a First Aid kit, some painkillers, anti-venom, but everything else is herbal. We raise the herbs we need to address health concerns. She should not have gotten sick from that water." The nun's mouth formed into a stubborn frown. "I think something else is wrong with her."

Cate's fury was evident. "Do not tell me you used the leaves from the *Caapi* plant to filter the water . . ."

The nun flushed. "Of course, I did. That's always what we use." Her eyes narrowed. "Again, that could not be what made her sick. It must have been something else."

Cate gazed at Anders. "*Caapi* is not only a hallucinogen, one of its side effects is projectile vomiting. If she's been vomiting over twenty-four hours, she's probably already dehydrated." Cate pressed a finger onto Dianna's forehead. It left a dent. She frowned. "We've got to get some real fluids into her and get the *Caapi* out of her system, *now*. Mark, in this environment, she could die. We've got to get her to an American embassy or at least an American doctor."

"You can't leave. Reverend John forbids it." The nun's words were firm.

Cate laughed. "Reverend John has no say in it. He's all tied up at the moment. Besides, we aren't part of your cult. We're merely volunteers, and we don't answer to the piss-wad who calls himself Reverend John." She nodded at Anders. "Mark, wrap her in a blanket and let's get her out of here. We need to get her airlifted to a place that actually practices medicine. Do you have transportation?"

Anders nodded. "Outside the gate."

"I know that there's some sort of military facility in Lima. That's probably your best bet."

Anders nodded again. "You're not coming with us?"

Cate shook her head. "I'll leave with your team. You'll get further, faster without me."

Anders nodded and began to bundle Dianna into a blanket.

The nun shook her head. "No." She said in a louder voice, "No!"

Anders glared at her. "Sorry, ma'am, you have no say."

The nun lunged for him, but the soldier grabbed her and forced her back into the chair. Cate swung at her, whacked her on the side of the head, and the women slid to the floor. Cate turned to Anders. "You go."

She gestured toward Anders' companions. "If someone raises an alarm, you'll have more than just the guards to worry about. That wacky tobacky everyone's ingesting keeps them within an inch of becoming unhinged." Cate frowned. "My dear Reverend brags about all the weapons he has stashed around here. Not sure what he's more worried about—the Apocalypse or his own followers."

At that moment, the lights went out. Cate chuckled. "Well, then. You blew the power grid? Great idea. Head straight down the hall and out the front door. The front gate is straight ahead." Anders hesitated. "*Go!*" Cate said.

Anders picked up Dianna and hurried out the door. He ran down the hallway, one armed soldier in front of him, the other behind. He hoped the rest of his team had done their jobs.

When they reached the main door of the mansion, the soldier in the lead kicked it open. Anders sprinted toward the gate.

Chapter Fifteen: Chaos

A s Anders and his two team members ran, a shot rang out, then another.

"They're not shooting at us, yet," one of the men shouted. "That came from within the mansion. One of the guys must have run into trouble."

Anders nodded. He was grateful that their Ninja suits deflected bullets, but they wouldn't protect Dianna. He pulled her body closer to his, trying to shield her. When they reached the front gate, two guards were sitting off to the side, bound and gagged. Another member of Anders' team stood over them. The man smirked. "Drunk as skunks. Easiest takedown ever."

Another shot rang out and punched through the gate, just over Anders' head. He ducked. The sound of running feet and enraged voices could be heard behind them. Someone pulled the gate open and Anders ran to a waiting Red Cross vehicle. Two men in scrubs placed Dianna on a stretcher and lifted the gurney into the back. Anders jumped in beside her. As more gunfire erupted, the medical personnel got into the vehicle and one of them yelled, "We've got to get out of here." The man in the passenger seat turned and gazed at Anders. "What do you know about the patient?"

Anders looked through the back window of the ambulance and watched several trucks unload troops. He turned to the two medics and growled. "She's not a patient, she's my wife. And I have no idea what the problem is, but they've been giving her *Caapi* and local water. She's been vomiting and is seriously dehydrated. Also hallucinating." He touched her forehead. "And now she's unconscious and burning up."

"Has she had all the required vaccinations?"

"Yes. She has the standard medical chip in her wrist, so you can verify."

"Probably poisoned her with their woo-woo shit. Damn locals think weeds are health food." The man turned to the driver. "George, pull over, man." He turned to Anders. "Sorry, you're going to have to trade places with me. Our instructions are to get you to La Paz and if need be, she's to be airlifted to one of the military installations in the region. But she needs fluids. I've got to start an IV."

The truck stopped and the man switched places with Anders. "I'm Medical Sergeant Cory Brandson, Special Forces, by the way. She's in good hands."

Anders nodded and climbed into the seat that had been vacated. He turned and tried to speak, but emotion overtook him. Finally, he managed to choke out, "I'm Agent Anders Mark. That's Agent Dianna Murphy. Help her." He buried his head in his hands and sobbed. *"Please."*

George punched the accelerator and said, "Roger, that!"

Cate peeked around the building that housed the Infirmary. The courtyard was filled with members of God's Delight, some bearing guns. A large horn blared and then someone using a megaphone said, "This is Carleton Smith with the American Red Cross. We have been authorized by the United Nations and our President to conduct a welfare check of all U.S. citizens residing within this compound. We are accompanied by U.N. Forces and the U.S. Military.

"We mean you no harm, I repeat, we mean you no harm. Please stand down. Our sole purpose is to verify the welfare of U.S. citizens. We ask that you drop your weapons and permit us to accomplish our purpose peacefully. Once we have completed the welfare check, we will leave. Again, please drop your weapons. Our intention is peaceful. However, we are authorized to use our weapons if threatened with deadly force."

Cate watched as the people with guns lined up in front of the gate, weapons drawn. *WTF?* Suddenly, another voice boomed out over the courtyard. "They're lying! They want to remove you forcefully from this compound and return you to your former lives. Do not let them take you!"

Heads began to nod, shouts of "They are the enemy!" could be heard.

"Protect yourselves," the voice urged. "Do not allow them to take you prisoner!"

Cate frowned. That couldn't be Reverend John. He was tied up by the communal bath. Who was speaking? It almost sounded like Fred, the guy from the cafeteria.

People began to move toward the gate as one. A shot was fired. Then another.

Cate scrunched her face in confusion. *Did these people have a death wish?* The gate was made of wood. It could hardly withstand a barrage of gunfire, from either direction. A scuffle off to the side caught Cate's attention. Several men dressed in the same black jumpsuits Mark Stiles wore appeared from the main building, bearing weapons. The courtyard was lit by a partial moon, permitting them to move through the crowd virtually unnoticed.

They lined up behind those bearing guns and one of them yelled, "Drop your weapons! You're surrounded."

Some of the people turned, their confusion clear. At that moment, the gates were torn open. A large spotlight bathed the compound in bright light. Over fifty people in riot gear moved into the courtyard. A battalion of men dressed in U.S.

military fatigues moved in behind them, guns drawn.

All hell broke loose. Several members of God's Delight began shooting, their bullets bouncing off the riot shields, ricocheting back into the crowd, striking several members of the mob. People screamed. Some panicked and turned to run. Suddenly, every single member of God's Delight that held a gun began shooting. That fire was returned.

Well, fuck a duck. Cate crouched to the ground, praying no bullets were aimed her way. She reached into the pocket of her robe and removed the pistol Mark had given her. She flicked off the safety with her thumb and knelt on the ground, waiting.

Finally, confident the situation in the courtyard was under control, Cate slipped away.

Tillie Spencer sat before the desk of her superior.

His bushy gray eyebrows were raised in a frown. He shook his head. "Really, Agent Spencer. Was it necessary to poison the American agent? She came close to losing her life."

Tillie nodded her head. "First of all, I didn't know she was an agent. She was just someone I connected with during the slave trafficking case. Both of us were kidnapped and put up for auction. She never once even hinted that she was on the job, so I did not probe.

"Yet, you both were using assumed names."

Tillie shrugged. "I'm sure she had her reasons, as did I."

The man's eyebrows crept up and his mouth opened to speak.

Tillie cut him off. "Second, I did what was expedient. I didn't know how else to avoid having her pulled into that creep's debauchery. He wanted her for himself. I thought it best to stop it before it started. That man takes. He doesn't ask permission."

The man gazed at her. "Yet, you managed to survive."

Tillie flushed. "Only because I knew what Reverend John was going in — the man is a sexual predator. I managed to avoid the worst of it." Tillie leaned forward, her expression earnest. "Look, I did what I thought best. Sometimes, the initiation for The Chosen involves a rather brutal gang bang. You're roofied and passed around. The harder you fight, the more dire the consequences. I had the antidote to the Rohypnol. I pretended to pass out quickly and they left me alone, mostly. But Dianna is a fighter. God knows what they would have done to break her."

The man studied her. "I see." He shifted his hefty form, sitting up straighter. "And where in the bloody hell did you find foxglove?"

"They had a massive herb garden. Tons of foxglove. I don't think they realized that in larger amounts, it was poisonous. It is often used for headaches, migraines and such. I simply slipped some into Dianna's coffee. Just enough to make her sick. Unfortunately, the nuns treated her with a combination of foxglove and *Caapi* tea. The foxglove never got a chance to pass through her system. It started to accumulate to toxic levels. She also had an allergic reaction to the *Caapi*. That just exacerbated her condition. It was a result I could not have anticipated, sir."

The man sighed. "Well, the Americans are pissed. I imagine you are now on their watch list." He tugged at his ear in irritation. "And what of our dear Anne?"

Tillie groaned. "The Countess managed to get herself in quite a pickle this time. She thought by offering herself to Reverend John, she could gain favor, be one of The Chosen. What she didn't realize is the Reverend was a taker. He was into force. Offering herself was a big mistake. He assigned her to the fields, manual labor. She became just another slave.

"She is very lucky his pockets were flush. The man is not above loaning out followers to some of the more popular brothels in the big cities as a way to raise cash."

A look of disgust crossed the man's face. "She's lucky all she suffered was the loss of her hair. You mentioned his interest in young girls in your report."

"The age of consent in that country is fourteen. He likes to initiate his adolescent followers into the sexual arts. He isn't much concerned about their age. And their parents consider it a privilege to have their child chosen. Serving him sexually is considered a privilege, not a punishment."

The man grunted. "That's sick. He chose the perfect country to indulge in that particular vice. Peru is known for trafficking in children. Tourists flock there for that reason."

Tillie nodded.

"Tell me about the attack and the welfare check."

"I was in another part of the mansion when the attack occurred, so I can only report what was told to me, sir."

"And that is?"

"As far as I could discern, the extraction team had secured Reverend John in the communal bath. Apparently, Sister Bethany went to look for him, gun in hand. She exchanged gunfire with the man holding him captive, accidentally striking Reverend John. She was shot dead. The Reverend was shot in the arm and back but survived. He came close to bleeding out." Tillie frowned. "Though as noted in the report, only one bullet came from Sister Bethany's gun. Where the other shot came from is a bit of a mystery. It did not come from any of the guns the Americans submitted to forensics."

The man cocked an eyebrow. "How odd. Any reports on his current condition?"

"He has recovered, sir. And he is using his survival as

proof of God's protection. If his people didn't believe in his omniscience before, they do now."

"Why wasn't he charged criminally?"

Tillie chuckled. "Surely you jest, sir. He may have lost a few members of his commune during the welfare check, but no one was willing to testify against him. Besides, he was renting his fields to a drug cartel. He was technically under their protection. With their money and their blessing, he is untouchable. However, the Americans have voided his passport. He is on the *Do Not Fly List* and has been banned from ever entering that country again. I suggest we do the same. Men like him don't give up, they just switch locations."

"How many others were injured?"

Tillie sighed. "When the dust cleared, forty-two members of God's Delight lay on the ground, dead or seriously wounded. One member of the U.N. International Peacekeeping Force died. After the tactical units took control, the followers threw down their weapons and surrendered."

"And the welfare check?"

"They rounded up almost one hundred sixty-five Americans, mostly students, but some who had been listed as missing persons in the states, a few on the run from law enforcement, and a few families who simply went off the grid. Eighty-three asked to leave. The others opted to stay."

The man frowned. "And what of the Brits?"

"Thirty-six total, twenty-five of whom asked to return home. We removed them immediately to the British Embassy for processing, including the Duchess."

"Any problems with removing those who asked to leave?"

Tillie shook her head. "There was no attempt to restrain them physically, but there was some public shaming. A lot of peer pressure to stay. I was amazed that we successfully removed as many as we did."

"So, what happens to those who stayed?"

"Apparently, life goes on, with Reverend John as their leader, sir." She pulled at on unseen thread on her skirt. "For some, having your free will compromised is a small price to pay when someone else will do all of your thinking for you. Plus, they aren't treated badly. They have food and shelter. They just have no real control over their lives. Different dreams, different destinies, I guess."

The man shook his head. "Well, I suppose a religious cult is preferred to joining a terrorist group, but personally, I would have a hard time handing responsibility for my well-being over to another. We didn't fight to be free to merely turn around and surrender that freedom to a third party."

Tillie gazed at the man. "And that, sir, is why you lead MISix, the one organization that protects this nation and its people at all costs."

"Indeed. What did you learn from this experience, Agent Spencer?"

Tillie reached into a pocket and removed a flash drive. She placed it on the man's desk. "Apparently, even con men who live in Third World countries profit. That includes the names of every single member who has joined the cult, the hackers they contracted with to wipe air travel and immigration records, and the drug cartels they do business with. It also provides a very nice record all other business interests. God's Delight is quite a profitable enterprise."

"We can work with that. I imagine you left a little something behind so we could back-door their systems if need be?"

Tillie nodded.

"Very good. Now, I really am curious. What has this experience taught you about cults?"

Tillie flushed. Then she said, "Those who can lead, do, sir.

And those who can't, follow. Sometimes, they join the military or a terrorist cell, and sometimes, they join a cult. It's a great repository for lost souls and people with bad judgment."

"That's an opinion I'd keep to myself, my dear. Comparing the military to a cult is a bit unseemly."

Tillie grinned. "Of course, sir. But something to think about. "So, what's next?"

"I'm afraid you're headed to Spain, Agent Spencer. Another royal is indulging in a walk on the wild side. He is out of control, and security concerns are involved. The Queen wants him retrieved and shipped to a treatment facility posthaste before he becomes a bargaining chip for those with less than commendable motives. Simply swoop in, scoop him up, and get him to the facility."

Tillie nodded. "Yes, sir." She stood. "I'll pick up my orders and leave today."

The man held up his hand. "And then take some time off, Agent Spencer. You were with that cult for six months, in deep cover. Two weeks spent being deprogrammed and weaned off *Caapi* hardly seems sufficient. The Americans put their agent in a month-long program, and she was at the compound less than a week. You may need more time to adjust."

Tillie flushed. "My understanding is that there were other issues with the agent. I'm fine, sir. Really."

The man harrumphed. "Regardless, go somewhere warm and sit on a beach for a week or two. I can't promise that your next assignment will be so easy."

Anders felt her stir before she awoke.

Slowly, he removed the arms he had carefully wrapped around Dianna while she slept and pulled himself from the hospital bed. Since they had returned from Peru a week ago, he had slept with her every night. It had taken almost three days for her dangerously high fever to break, and when it did, Dianna was so weak she could barely communicate. It wasn't until the night before that she had opened her still-glazed blue eyes and recognized him.

Dianna stirred again and yawned. Her eyelids fluttered. She smiled at Anders. "Where are we?" she asked.

"At Milwaukee Medical. We had to evacuate you from Peru. You got really sick. After they got you stabilized at a military base in Lima, Sheikh Ali sent a plane and we brought you home. Do you remember anything?"

Dianna cleared her throat. "Water?" Anders handed her a cup with a straw and she sipped. "The last thing I remember is being told the bus wasn't working. I was offered a tour of the compound. I thought it was strange, because Cate was gone and so were the other girls. But the woman who asked was Tillie, the MISix agent I told you about." She paused and sipped some more. "I ate lunch with the other people at the compound and got really sleepy, so I took a nap. Then things got weird."

"Weird how?"

"I started to feel like I was losing my grip on reality, as if I was floating outside of myself. I even had a dream about Reverend John dancing naked while playing with a viper. The crowd was frenzied. Like they were on drugs or something."

Anders took her hand and stroked it. "Sadly, from what former cult members have told us, the snake thing may have been real. Reverend John likes to play with snakes, similar to Pentecostal rituals. He used them to convince his followers that he had some sort of sacred dispensation, though we suspect the snakes he used were venomoids. Snakes with their venom removed. Just all part of the theatre that is Reverend John." Anders frowned. "You were hallucinating when we got to you, though, so we may never know what you actually witnessed."

Dianna yawned. "What about the snakes in that viper's pit? Were they venomoids, too? Everyone seemed terrified of them."

Anders chuckled. "Nope. That was his own version of that old TV show, *Fear Factor*. Some of the locals enjoyed the challenge of being hung upside down in the well. It was all a game. Tempt the snakes and get out. Great entertainment for those who like that sort of thing."

Dianna frowned. "That's sick . . ."

Anders snorted. "Not much else to do in the middle of the jungle, I guess." He stroked her cheek. "Do you remember anything else? You were there for four days. You've only mentioned two."

Dianna shook her head. "I don't know what was real and what wasn't. I need time to sort it all out." She groaned and rubbed her stomach. "I feel like crap," she murmured.

A doctor in bright pink scrubs walked in. She turned on her notepad and studied it. Then she studied Dianna. "Well, we've got your test results back. You're a lucky woman. Your blood was loaded with all kinds of shit. They found a hallucinogen called *Caapi*." The doctor frowned. "And high levels of foxglove, usually used to treat headaches, but also toxic if ingested regularly."

Dianna frowned. "I was pretty careful about what I ate and drank."

The doctor shrugged. "The natives consider *Caapi* a health food. They put it in everything—food, tea, cigarettes. You're allergic to it."

"But why did I have a fever? Allergies don't cause fevers, do they?"

"Given the high level of foxglove in your system, I suspect your body was reacting to its toxicity. Intentionally or unintentionally, you were being poisoned."

"That makes no sense. Why?"

The doctor shook her head. "I'm afraid that's above my pay grade." She walked to Dianna and checked her pulse, then listened to her heart. She studied the monitors next to Dianna's bed. "We've been pumping you with fluids to force all the bad stuff out of you. It seems to be working. Your vitals are improving. How do you feel, really?"

"Like I've been run over by a truck."

The doctor frowned. "You might be going into some sort of withdrawal. *Caapi* is very addictive. Sometimes, the body embraces it quickly and craves it, even if you're allergic to it. Eventually, your system would have adjusted and the allergy would have subsided." She cocked an eyebrow. "I'm afraid standard protocol is a mandatory thirty-day stay in rehab for detox, deprogramming, and other issues. Also, your superiors are worried about some panic attacks you had. That requires a mandatory psych eval. You'll have to be cleared before returning to active duty."

Dianna groaned. "That sucks."

The doctor winked. "If you cooperate, you might get conjugal visits."

Anders laughed. "Trust me. I'll make sure she cooperates."

The doctor smiled at Anders. "I think he's a keeper."

EPILOGUE

Dianna cradled the tiny baby in her arms and cooed. She smiled at Janet. "She's so beautiful. And she looks just like you."

Cade laughed. "Thank God. I'd hate to have my daughter stuck with this ugly mug." He pointed at his face.

Janet swatted at him. "Oh, stop it. Until she grows into her looks, we'll have no idea who she resembles. Look at Ethan. He's almost three, and already we have photos where he looks like you, then me, and now, my father. Besides, it doesn't matter who she looks like." She reached for her daughter. "She's our little sweet pea." She extended a finger and the baby grabbed it. Janet winced. "She already has Daddy's strength. She's got a grip like a vise."

Dianna laughed. She nudged Anders. "Can't wait until we have one of our own."

Anders blushed. "Well, that's kind of why we're here today, isn't it?"

Dianna sighed. "Yup. So, let's get this over with." She gazed at Cade. "I had a lot of time to think in rehab. The doctors can't guarantee the panic attacks won't reoccur. And I'm still having nightmares. How can I trust myself to have Anders' back in the field when I'm not one hundred percent? We all know any distraction is dangerous. I would rather work behind the scenes than put my husband's life and mine at risk."

Cade smiled. "I trust your judgment. If and when you feel ready to return to the field, we'll revisit the issue. For now, I like the idea of you transitioning into training. You'll be great at it. You have patience, skill, and a way with people. When Hope Ali finally gets her act together and comes on board, I think you'd be the perfect person to oversee her development. She respects you, and unlike me and Anders, she'll listen to you. So will other recruits. But I have another proposal. An additional task I'd like you to take on—Janet's old job."

Dianna cocked an eyebrow. "Hacking computers?"

Janet grinned. "Among other things. I'll need to train you as a locksmith and safecracker as well."

A puzzled expression crossed Dianna's face. "But my intent is to pull back from fieldwork."

Cade nodded. "And you will. You'll act more as a resource. When agents need assistance in those areas, we now have the ability to aid them remotely. They can turn control of computers—any electronic device really—over to you via the Agency cloud. You'll have a direct com link in real time."

Janet stood and began to rock the baby in her arms. "I'm taking a year's maternity leave from the law school, so it will be a good time for the transition." She kissed Chloe's head as the baby began to doze. "Ethan and Chloe will keep me busy, but Ethan's starting pre-school next year, so I'll be available almost whenever you need me."

She studied Dianna. "You're sure you're ready for a desk job?"

Dianna laughed. "Training won't exactly have me tied to a desk. There will be plenty of field trips, tests of skills out in the real world. Obstacle courses. Other drills. I just want to control the risk as much as I can." She shook her head. "If Anders hadn't extracted me when he did, I wouldn't be here . . ."

"Coming so close to death is kind of a wake-up call, isn't it?" Janet asked. "It forces you to get your priorities in order."

Dianna nodded. "And danger and death are not among them." She patted Anders' arm affectionately. "I want to stay with the Agency, but I felt totally out of control in Peru. I do not want to go through that again, ever." She leaned over and kissed Anders. "And I don't think it's fair to put Anders through that either."

Cade grunted. "But it's okay if he puts you through it?"

Dianna shrugged. "I guess my priorities are different. My work is not what defines me. I need to feel useful, to make a contribution, but I'm not an action junkie. My husband is." She grinned at Janet. "I've always envied you. You seem to have your life all figured out. I guess now it's time for me to do the same."

Cade smirked. "You might change your mind after training Hope. That kid has a way of . . ."

Dianna laughed. "Look, I know Hope is a sneaky little shit. If she can find a shortcut, she'll take it. But she's also smart, and mostly, reasonable. When she outgrows her adolescent impulsiveness, she will make a good agent. In fact, I think she'll be one of the best. Maybe we'll learn from each other."

Janet laughed. "Ok, then. Welcome to my world."

"I do have some questions about the God's Delight case, though. I read the report, but some information is missing. And Anders wasn't very forthcoming."

Cade cocked an eyebrow. "Such as?"

"Well, for one thing, what happened to Cate? Hope said she'd cleared out of the apartment. Just up and disappeared. Anders told me what she did for me. I want to thank her."

Cade grinned. "Cate is taking some time off to rethink her priorities. She may be joining the Agency."

"But she isn't a lawyer. Heck, she flunked out of . . ."

Cade snickered.

"What?" Dianna asked.

"Great cover, wasn't it?"

Dianna frowned. "What?"

"Cate was working for someone else. She's a very talented actress."

"So, she's not some promiscuous debutante?"

Cade laughed. "Need to know. Sorry. You can ask her if she signs on. Because you'll be training her, too."

"Did we at least find Merry Wright?"

"No. God's Delight claims she was never a member. And we have no real proof to the contrary. We're still looking, but she could be anywhere. People go off the rails every day and simply disappear. Some don't want to be found. With no proof she actually left the country, we're at a dead end, for now."

"What about the frat connection, Tau Omega Psi?"

Cade smirked. "Now that's an interesting story." Cade sat in an armchair and picked up his son, Ethan, who had been coloring in a book on the floor. "Apparently, GoFlex Foundation is a corporate sponsor of student missionary trips. It's funded with donations from corporations who desire to support religious causes without the public flack. Thus, the generic name. Essentially, the group believes the younger generation lacks the motivation to do good works in Third World countries, so it funds missionary trips, utilizing fraternities and sororities interested in public service projects. Obviously, the hope is that students will stay, one day return as volunteers, or become donors."

"Nothing wrong with that."

Cade tickled his son and smiled. "Except GoFlex tends to freely to grant money, ask questions later. You've met Mike Addison, one of the guys who organized your trip. He's a former roadie for the God's Delight college campus tour. When he quit and decided to go to UW, Reverend John asked him to organize a couple of mission trips that could introduce students to the God's Delight compound. Specifically, Reverend John asked for young women. Candidates for The Chosen. The good Reverend even hooked him up with GoFlex for funding."

Janet rocked Chloe, smiling down at her daughter's sleeping face. "When the students got down there, Mike made sure the prettiest women were diverted to the compound, on the pretense of a housing shortage."

"And what? They just left them there?"

Janet shook her head. "After Reverend John had a chance to sample the goods, so to speak, he would sometimes make one of the women an offer he thought they couldn't refuse. Some women bought it, some didn't. Regardless, the rest of the women were also introduced to the cult and invited to stay. That kind of culture attracts a certain type of person. Some women did join, willingly. Mike was supposed to notify their families of their decision, but the guy's a slacker. He didn't."

Cade laid his son down gently on his lap as Ethan dozed off. "So, Mike was essentially acting as a procurer, a pimp, as well as a recruiter. The problem was, while decisions to stay were made freely, once in, it wasn't easy to get out. You saw where that group is located. It's isolated. Even if someone walked through those gates, they had nowhere to go. As we discovered during the welfare check, more than a few wanted to go home but had no way to get there. God's Delight wasn't exactly providing return tickets."

"What about the other guys, Alex in particular? Did he know?"

Cade shook his head. "Not that we could prove. Remember, that was his first trip down there. We could find no reason to believe he knew what was going on, and if other fraternity members did, they aren't talking."

Anders set down the beer he was drinking and asked, "So what? They all just walk away Scott-free?"

Cade laughed. "Not exactly. The fraternity's charter has been suspended by the University, pending further investigation. When the group returned from Bolivia—minus Cate, Dianna, the other three women, and of course, Anders—Alex was told that all of the women had decided to stay, and that Anders had been turned over to a representative of the U.S. Embassy in Bolivia, since he didn't have a passport. The F.B.I. was at the Milwaukee airport to greet them. Everyone who went on the trip was questioned. Ultimately, Mike was arrested for slave trafficking. Forced labor, the category the cult members were ultimately placed in since the sex appeared to be consensual, is still slavery. He pled out, but not before spilling his guts. He gave us enough to arrest and convict Reverend John and The Chosen, but only in the U.S. And we can't get out hands on him. Peru refuses to extradite."

Dianna asked, "What about the women from other campuses. Same tactics?"

Janet sighed. "Apparently, there are few other Mikes out there. The F.B.I. is still investigating."

Dianna frowned. "That's a lot of women for one man."

Janet smirked. "Apparently, Reverend John prefers to lead a flock of women. He believes women are easier to manipulate. You may have noticed the lack of men in the compound. Most are locals or men hiding from law enforcement—mercenaries or other undesirables."

Dianna shook her head. She reached over and stroked Chloe's hair. "Did Anders tell you about the guy from GoFlex on the plane? He appeared to be designating the woman to be delivered to Reverend John."

Anders nodded. "I did tell them. Problem is, the guy claims he was counting the number of women on the trip and expressing concern about adequate accommodations. The guys backed him up."

Dianna emitted an exasperated sigh. "So, everyone but Mike walks free? How is that justice? Surely we can get Reverend John on slave trafficking as well?"

Cade scowled. "Therein lies the problem. Peru is known for trafficking in humans—men, women, and children—for all sorts of reasons. Some are forced into labor for the drug cartels, as well as more legitimate enterprises, such as mining, logging, and agriculture. Others are forced into domestic servitude for the upper classes or fed into the sex trades, not only prostitution but also child sex tourism. Reverend John's little experiment in human slavery is nothing compared to other groups operating in that country. He's small potatoes. In addition, he's protected by the drug cartels. He rents them land to grow poppies for the heroin trade. He chose the location of his compound wisely. We can't touch him, and the Peruvian authorities have no desire to."

Cade picked up his sleeping son and stood. "Unless he tries to sneak back into the U.S., our hands are tied."

"The trip wasn't a total loss," Janet said. "We were able to do a welfare check. We did remove people who wanted to return home. It's a small victory, but sometimes, it's the small ones that make the greatest difference.

"Every humanitarian and watch group in the world knows what God's Delight is now. The U.N. has made sure of that. Knowledge is power. Sometimes, that's our best weapon."

You may also enjoy the following from eXtasy Books Inc:

Kinky Briefs
Seelie Kay

Excerpt

There was no question that I had won. The evidence I presented left the jury as well as most of the gallery in tears. There was nothing the defense could offer that would refute my case.

I was about to move for a directed verdict when the judge slammed down his gavel and ordered all the parties and counsel into his chambers. As we crowded into his office, I maneuvered my client's wheelchair before the judge's desk. I shot opposing counsel a defiant glare. This was a case that should never have seen the inside of the courtroom.

A year ago, Elsa Tangine left a luncheon at the local country club, drunk. It was not an unusual state for the pretty trophy wife. She had wrangled out of five DUIs and had another one pending. This time, however, she broadsided my client, Dean Johnson, leaving him a paraplegic with limited brain function. Once a talented and successful civil engineer, Dean now huddled in a wheelchair, attended by a nursing assistant.

Dean's future was destroyed in a single selfish moment. My client's mind was muddled and his speech impaired. The medical bills were mounting, and without an income, he was about to lose his lovely country home. The destruction silly little Elsa had wreaked was total and complete.

After the annoying deposition, which uncovered nothing that would aid the defense, Elsa's husband decided to fight our lawsuit anyway. One way or another, he knew his wife was going down, and he did not wish to go down with her. Brock Tangine hired two of the country's leading defense attorneys. One was a civil attorney, assigned the task of limiting the damages in the current case. The other was a criminal attorney, hoping to minimize evidence that could put his client in prison.

Insurance counsel was reduced to third chair, and he appeared to be relieved.

The judge removed his robe and sat down in his grand leather maroon office chair. He clasped his hands in front of him. Everyone shifted uneasily in their chairs as his piercing gaze swept the room. It was clear he intended to show no mercy. Finally, his eyes settled on Elsa.

"Young lady," he thundered. "You are a menace to society, and if I had the power, I would throw you in jail for all of your natural life. You are a drunk. Why have you not sought treatment? You can certainly afford it."

Elsa burst into tears, a tactic that had probably brought more than one man to his knees. The judge, however, did not appear moved. He waited impatiently for her answer, but she said nothing.

The judge refocused his attention on opposing counsel, in particular, the highly-paid defense attorneys. "Gentlemen," he said. "You are wasting the time and the resources of this court. You cannot possibly defend this case. You cannot possibly win. I can only assume that you and your client have some sort of sadistic desire to punish the plaintiff for pursuing this thoroughly justified complaint."

The civil attorney started to open his mouth, but a sharp elbow to his side from the criminal defense lawyer silenced him.

The judge waited a minute, apparently unsure if the other attorneys had the good judgment to remain silent. Finally, he said, "I want a settlement in this case, and I want it quickly."

He looked at me and asked, "What is your target offer. What will you accept?"

I looked at my client and placed my hand on his. I wanted everyone to feel this man's pain. Slowly, I responded, "I intend to ask the jury for twenty million in damages, and another twenty-five million in punitive damages, Your Honor. The defense and the defendant have acted with malice and have continually attempted to subvert justice. My client can never be made whole, but he can be provided with sufficient funds to ease his pain and live out his life as comfortably as possible."

Elsa and her attorneys gasped. Insurance counsel said, "Your Honor, the defendant's insurance will cover only a very small portion of the requested damages. The rest will have to come out of the defendant's pocket."

The judge smiled. "Not my problem," he replied. "That's your monkey. I suggest you accept plaintiff's terms. I suspect the jury will at least double it. Did you see the tears? The total disdain they have for your client?"

The defense settled that day. Insurance counsel delivered the check to my office three days later. The chicken-shit high-powered defense attorneys fled town shortly thereafter. While Brock Tangine fought payment, the judge made it clear he had no choice. He was informed in open court that his failure to address his wife's drinking problem could be construed as contributory negligence, and the judge would happily entertain a motion to amend the lawsuit and add him as a party.

I accepted the check graciously. My client would be well-cared for his entire natural life, and that was gratifying.

Opposing counsel asked, "How much of the check will you pocket?"

I glared at him. Finally, I responded, "Five percent. I wasn't about to take any more than required to compensate for my time."

Counsel came around my desk and began massaging my shoulders. "Always the bleeding heart, darling," he said. He reached down and pulled my blouse out of my skirt. His hand disappeared underneath. He yanked down my bra and stroked my nipples. "Where shall we go to celebrate?" he asked.

About the Author

Seelie Kay writes about lawyers in love, with a dash of kink.

Writing under a nom de plume, the former lawyer and journalist draws her stories from more than 30 years in the legal world. Seelie's wicked pen has resulted in many works of fiction, including the Kinky Briefs series, the Feisty Lawyers series, The Garage Dweller, A Touchdown to Remember, The President's Wife, The President's Daughter, and Seizing Hope, and as well as the erotic romance anthology, Pieces of Us.

When not spinning her kinky tales, Seelie ghostwrites nonfiction for lawyers and other professionals. Currently, she resides in a bucolic exurb outside Milwaukee, WI, where she shares a home with her son and enjoys opera, the Green Bay Packers, gourmet cooking, organic gardening, and an occasional bottle of red wine.

Seelie is an MS warrior and ruthlessly battles the disease on a daily basis. Her message to those diagnosed with MS: Never give up. You define MS, it does not define you!

Seelie can be reached at www.seeliekay.com, www.seeliekay.blogspot.com, or on Twitter or Facebook.